Gus

Good God but the man was a scrumptious treat.

That was my one pervasive thought as I enjoyed my break from the pediatrics unit by catching up on my favorite food vlogger. He made some type of Asian style fish with soy sauce and lemons, and hand-made noodles, and the whole image of him holding the bowl with one hand, chopsticks in the other, I didn't know which looked better.

The man or the food.

Too bad in real life, Antonio Ricci was everything a sensible woman wouldn't want in a man. Oh, he was wonderful with his daughter Rosie, who was the very definition of adorable, but he as also the walking, talking embodiment of a bad boy. A heartbreaker. Even while doing something as utterly domestic as making a meal, he looked like he just walked out of some woman's bedroom and straight into his kitchen. His hair was always mussed like a woman had run her fingers through it in the throes of ecstasy, his arms were heavily muscled and full of colorful tattoos, the black t-shirts he favored clung to his arms and shoulders like a lover reluctant to let him go, and sweet lord in heaven, that sexy smirk he always flashed at the camera was enough to dampen a girl's panties.

Including mine.

I was sure, despite having no evidence, that there was a string of broken hearts in his wake. Around Jackson's Ridge, he was the favored son who'd done well and returned home for the sake of his daughter. The good guy, the chef everyone loved. But that was a façade. It had to be right? No man that gorgeous and that talented was as good as the town thought he was.

Not that it mattered to me because I just liked to look at Antonio while he taught me how to cook delicious meals from around the world.

End of story.

The door to the break room squeaked and I felt myself tense, because it was either someone who would want to talk, or worse, I was being called back to work seven minutes into my break. Melanie Gibson, head nurse for Jackson's Ridge Medical Center, peeked her head in with a smile and the most knowing set of blue eyes in all of Oregon.

"There you are, Gus," she trilled as if she didn't know exactly where I was at all times when I was on the premises. "You're needed in exam room four."

We were in the business of helping people, and that came first. Above meals and bathroom breaks, breakdowns, personal drama and pretty much everything else. Still, a girl had to protect her mental health, didn't she?

"My break just started. Where's Sally?"

Melanie pushed the door open and fisted her hands at her hips, just in case there was any confusion over how she felt about my answer. She stared me down until I felt myself start to shrink. Too bad it wasn't my ass or my hips or my belly shrinking, or else I might not have cared.

"You have a patient Gus."

I took one last look at Antonio's charming smirk and groaned. Melanie was right, of course, and I loved my job as a pediatric nurse. It was my job to make the little ones comfortable and confident during what could be a scary time for them. I loved their wide-eyed wonder when they felt better, when they realized a treatment was working, and most of all, when they got a cast put on for the first time. It was adorable and heartwarming, making my days at work more rewarding than I'd ever imagined.

"All right, all right," I slipped my phone into the pocket of my pink and purple scrubs, mismatched thanks to an eight year old who got into his daddy's beer. "I'm on my way to exam room four."

Melanie flashed a satisfied smile. "Excellent. Thank you, Gus."

I took a few minutes to wash my hands and rinse my mouth before making my way to the exam room which was reserved for patients without an appointment and who didn't require emergency services. I sucked in a deep breath and pasted on a smile as I reached for the chart and stepped inside the room. It was important to keep things positive with pediatric patients—and their parents—because the former listened better and the latter panicked less.

I blinked and opened my mouth to start my usual spiel, but my mouth wouldn't work because it had gone instantly dry at the sight of Antonio lounging in the blue plastic chair. Even though there was very little variety in his wardrobe—black, white or gray t-shirts, jeans always, and boots or sneakers depending on the day—he was always breathtaking. Especially up close. I gave myself a mental chastising and relaxed my shoulders as I focused on the chart until I felt normal again.

"Mr. Ricci and Little Ms. Ricci, hi. What brings you in today?" There, that sounded normal. Totally normal.

Antonio flashed a sexy grin and sat forward to lean his elbows on his knees. "Just a check up to make sure the treatments are working."

Yes, multiple treatments because little Rosie had an awful case of chronic severe asthma. They'd tried everything to get her attacks under control and it seemed over the past six months or so, something had worked. I nodded and turned my attention to Rosie.

"How have you been feeling lately?"

Rosie sat a little taller, clearly feeling like a big girl as she straightened her orange and blue jeweled crown with a shy smile. The little girl opened her mouth to answer, when a deeper voice intruded. "She's had a bit of a chest rattle, but only after she's been running around."

I turned with a glare for the handsome chef. "It's not your turn, Dad. First let Rosie tell me in her own words how she feels." His nostrils flared at the challenge in my tone, and I arched my brows daring him to argue with me before I turned my attention back to Rosie. "Well, how have you been feeling?"

Rosie nodded and her big brown eyes focused on me, serious and thoughtful. "Sometimes it's hard to breathe when I play tag or kickball, but I'm fine when I play princess. Do you like princesses?"

I smiled at the question. It was no secret how much little Rosie loved princesses. "What's not to like? Beautiful dresses, gorgeous jewels and parties all the time. Sounds like a pretty ideal life to me." Especially compared to the childhood I'd actually had.

"Yeah," she sighed wistfully.

The heat of Antonio's gaze on the side of my face was distracting as hell, and I knew I had to get the appointment back on track. "What about when you're sleeping, Rosie, do you ever wake up out of breath?"

She snuck a glance at her father and then back to me with a nod. "Sometimes. It's scary at first, but then it goes away fast."

"Are you having bad dreams or exciting dreams?"

Antonio sat up straight, as eager for the answer as I was. A slow grin bloomed across Rosie's pale face. "Exciting!" She leaned forward as if she was sharing a secret. "Sometimes I ride dragons or fight giants, and one time I rode a whale to rescue the king!"

My eyes went wide at the tomboy princess before me. She had an active imagination that probably developed from all the time spent inside the walls of hospitals and doctor's offices. "Well that explains it. Those exciting dreams of yours are no different from running and playing outside, so maybe try to dream about going for long walks around the castle grounds before bed, and leave the dragon rides for the daytime when someone can keep an eye on you, yeah?"

She let out a huff of disappointment and nodded. "Okay. I will. Promise."

"I'll hold you to that promise," I told her and busied myself with checking her vitals and listening to her breathing.

"Do you hear the rattle? It's slight, but it's

there." Antonio's question came from right next to my ear, and a second later I felt the heat of his body against my back. The scent of garlic and spices wafted to my nose, and I turned to glare at him.

"Can't hear anything with you growling in my ear."

He smiled and took a step back, not looking even a little bit sorry for invading my space. "I don't growl, that's just what my voice sounds like."

I documented Rosie's vitals, and straightened to standing. "Everything looks good, Rosie. I'll let the doctor know that you're ready for him." I tried for a smile, but it faltered under the weight of Antonio's glare. "Take care, Rosie."

"You too, Nurse Gus!" she gave an energetic wave that only little kids could manage which I returned, and then I got the hell out of the exam room before I said something I might have to apologize for later.

Out in the hall, I let out a deep breath and turned to return the chart to the holder mounted on the wall. I felt Antonio behind me and I let out another deep breath, prepared for whatever perceived infraction I committed this time. Parents were the worst part of pediatrics.

"What can I do for you, Mr. Ricci?"

He blinked in surprise, but it didn't stop the way his nostrils flared or the anger burning in 'his eyes. "Look, Nurse Thompson, I don't appreciate-,"

"The name is Gus or August." I cut him off just to, I don't know, piss him off further or cool his anger.

Antonio mentally stumbled at the interruption and raked a hand through his already mussed hair to gather his thoughts again. Sometimes I watched him do that and wondered if he did it just to increase his sex appeal for his videos.

"Fine, *Augusta*. I don't appreciate you cutting me off when I'm telling you what's wrong with my kid."

I nodded, because I understood where he was coming from, but I didn't back down when it came to my patients. Ever. "Noted. I don't appreciate you butting in when I'm asking *the patient* a question about their health."

His brown eyes widened in shock, maybe it was outrage. "Patient? She's five, what the hell does she know about her health?"

Typical parent. "Did you know she woke up with breathing difficulties sometimes?" The look of helpless-ness on his face told me he hadn't known. "Right. She's five today, but one day soon she'll be twelve and then fifteen and twenty-three, and *she* will need to know how to manage her sickness for herself. She needs to know how to identify when something is wrong or when she's fine. This is her illness," my voice softened with under-standing because I really did understand where he was coming from, "even though it doesn't feel like it, Mr. Ricci. It's never too early to start giving Rosie some autonomy over her condition." I let out a slow breath and arched a brow at him. Parents always had more to say and they always had to have the final word, and I was happy to let them vent when it was appropriate. "Anything else?"

Antonio surprised me when he shook his head and took a step back.

I took advantage of regaining the ability to breath again and walked away, hoping like hell he wasn't staring at the purple scrub pants I wore that were a little too snug in the thighs.

Antonio

✾

ugusta Thompson was a knockout. And a smartass. The latter didn't prevent me from enjoying the former, because I stared for a long time as she marched away from me, probably calling me every name in the book in her head as she did so. He purple scrub pants were just tight enough to let me appreciate the roundness of her ass, the slight jiggle that made my fingers itch to touch it. The soft thighs I had too many fantasies about parting with my hips. My shoulders.

Damn those curves, they haunted me with every trip I made to this medical center, which was too often for my liking.

But the smartass made a good point about Rosie. I needed to let my daughter speak for herself when she could. I knew that. Augusta wasn't the first person to tell me that. In fact, my sister Teddy and my older brother Vincenzo said the same thing to me on a regular basis, but I didn't want to hear it. It had taken a long time to get a handle on her constant asthma attacks, and now that we had it under control, they couldn't just expect me to take a step back.

I hated that Augusta had made a good point, but I hated it more that I didn't have a ready comeback for the know-it-all nurse.

Next time, Augusta.

"Something wrong, Antonio?"

I turned at the sound of Dr. Knox's voice and shook my head. "Nah, just another run-in with Augusta."

He let out a booming laugh and shook his head, opening the exam room door with a nod for me to enter first. "You two will figure it out. Eventually."

I ignored that and took a seat beside Rosie, waiting to hear what the doctor had to say. "Anything I need to worry about?"

"Nothing at all," he assured both of us with a smile. "Rosie is responding to treatment in just the way we were hoping. There will be small flare ups on occasion, but as long as you can identify them and treat them in a timely fashion, Rosie will be fine."

Fine. For most people it was such a small word, such a little thing to hope for, especially when it came to a child as lively as Rosie. But she hadn't been fine back in Los Angeles, and it turns out that it was more than the clean, crisp Oregon air that was responsible for her improved health. It was Dr. Knox. And yeah, it was also Augusta. The medical staff and my family, they were the dream team that would help me keep Rosie healthy and happy. That was my only goal when I packed up our lives and moved back to Jackson's Ridge.

Not many men would give up a career that was on the rise as a celebrity chef to become what was basically a glorified vlogger. Sure, I was one of the most popular YouTubers within the home cooks sphere, and I had a best-selling cookbook, not to mention guest spots on morning talk shows at the local and national level. The success was a good thing, but it wasn't working in a kitchen. It wasn't making sous chefs shake in their chef's whites for not meeting my exacting expectations. It wasn't creating menus that critics said made me a culinary genius. The photo shoots and endorsement deals were still there, but they just weren't the same.

But I'd given Los Angeles a solid shot when Rosie's health started to fade. I tried for twelve long, arduous months, visiting specialist after specialist, trying any and every new drug promised to work wonders against the plagues of asthma. But none of it had made a difference, so I'd moved back home, and this was my life now. Cooking and being the best damn dad I could.

Every sacrifice was well worth it to see my little girl so happy and so full of life. It was better than catching her wheezing on the sofa, struggling to breathe. And being surrounded by my three brothers and my sister Teddy, meant she had plenty of adults who thought she was just as wonderful as I did, something every kid should have in their lives. Lots of love and attention.

"Daddy's daydreaming again!" Rosie's words pulled me from thoughts of the past, from my nonstop, dissatisfied career musings. "Are you listening, Daddy?"

I blinked away the image of Rosie struggling for breath when I walked into my ex-wife's apartment more than two years ago. Her face was a terrifying mix of pale white and sickly green, her brown eyes filled with fear and hope that I would be able to ease her pain, stop her fear. I turned with a smile towards Rosie.

"Of course I am. Don't you recognize my listening face?" My brows dipped low and I put my chin on top of my fist, leaning forward until she giggled.

That sound, it was the sound of a happy child, a little girl who knew she was loved. And each time I heard it, I knew moving back home had been the right choice.

Gus

❦

"Put those wine bottles in the canvas bag, please." The bag boy pretended not to hear me, but the way he grunted told me he'd heard me just fine, that and the overly dramatic way he removed all three bottles from the bags and put them in one bag. "Thank you."

"Whatever," he practically growled at me.

"Nice manners," I shot back and pushed my cart away, deciding that his snotty attitude did not warrant the tip he would have gotten for helping me load the bags into the trunk. I was an able-bodied woman, sure my able body had a little too much cushion in certain spots, but I was working on it, and I was perfectly capable of loading my own groceries. And unloading them.

For the past few months I was doing double shopping duty on my days off, picking up enough food for me and for my father to last at least a few days, if not a full week. One of my biggest victories of the past year was convincing him to move to Jackson's Ridge so we could work on our strained relationship. Even though he had given up the bottle more than a decade ago, we were both too stubborn to let go of the past before now.

You're probably asking yourself what in the hell *he* had to be upset about, well that was *my* question at first too. It turns out that being a self-sufficient daughter of an alcoholic made one insufferable. That's right, he was upset with me for taking care of him and myself when I was just a kid. It had taken a few months to get used to being in each other's lives again, but now we could at least be in the same room without fighting.

Bickering, yes. Fighting, no.

"Who told you it was all right to just walk inside my house?" Dad's voice rang out with the crystal clarity I'd never heard in my childhood, but the grumpy tone I remembered well. "What if I was entertaining a woman in here?"

I stood between his oversized recliner and his oversized television, blocking his early afternoon entertainment, arms full of groceries for him.

"Then I would have gotten quite an eyeful, but you know Dad, it wouldn't be the first time I caught you having sex." It happened on a regular basis after Mom split, a revolving door of drunken bar bunnies who didn't care who they took home or went home with, as long as they didn't end the night alone. Dad was happy to oblige, because it gave him a drinking and sex partner for the night. And me, well I was just happy he made it home safely every night. "I've caught more than my fair share of older couples getting it on in the hospital. Must be something about dodging death that gets them all hot and bothered."

Dad's lips twitched even as he tried to narrow his gaze for another glare. Eventually, the smile came, slow and wide. "Who you callin' old?" He pushed his lanky frame up from the recliner and took the bags from my hand.

"If the grey fits, old man." He barked out a laugh and set the bags down on the kitchen table with a fake grunt. "Do you even know any ladies to entertain?" As far as I knew, he hadn't dated since moving to Jackson's Ridge nearly a year ago.

Oliver Thompson was as stubborn as the day was long, and I knew he wouldn't answer the question. "That's not proper talk for fathers and daughters," he admonished with a frown.

"It is when they are both adults, so tell me about all these women you entertain while I'm busy working."

"I can do my own shopping these days, Augusta." Avoidance had always been one of his favorite strategies to get out of difficult conversations, and this time I let it slide.

"I'm well aware of that, Dad. But I also know you'll end up with a fridge full of frozen meals, chips and every flavor of soda the grocery store has to offer."

Dad rolled his eyes and folded his arms while he fixed me with a glare only a father could produce. "That was one damn time, and only because they were on sale, five bottles for five bucks. That's ten liters of pop for a fiver, little girl and where I come from that's considered a deal."

Not when you factor in the dental costs that will come later, or buying bigger pants. Or diabetes medication."

He waved off my concerns. "You worry too much, Gus."

"Maybe you worry too little. It's a known fact that single men don't take care of themselves and married men live longer."

His green eyes, just a smidge lighter than my own, went wide and he let out a loud, guffawing laugh. "Now you're trying to marry me off? What the hell, girl?"

"I'm not trying to marry you off, Dad. I just want to keep you healthy." I put a few items in the fridge and groaned. "I'll stop doing groceries for you when you start buying things like fruits and vegetables."

He scoffed. "Damn things taste like cardboard."

"They do not! You ate three helpings of broccoli mac & cheese last week."

He smiled. "Yeah that was good, even with the broccoli in it."

"Then this discussion is over."

He grumbled his disapproval and reached inside the fridge for the apple juice I just put in there. "You staying for lunch today?" He asked the same question each time I stopped by with groceries, and every time, without fail, I felt a little warmth in my chest that he actually wanted me around now.

"Yep. I thought we could try something new today."

Dad dropped down onto one of the wooden kitchen stools and sighed. "What is it this time? Raw butterfly stomachs with a ketchup aioli?"

"Ew, gross."

"Well, I dunno with all the strange foods you force me to eat these days. You on some kind of cleanse?"

"Strange? Is that why you eat until your belly aches?"

He shrugged. "I didn't say it wasn't good, I said it was strange." His lips twitched again and I shook my head.

"It's called char Siu." I had saved Antonio's step-by-step video from last week and bought all the ingredients today. It looked simple enough, I was confident I could manage. "It's Asian and it's pork, but what you'll love most is that you get to fire up the grill." I couldn't help but smile when Dad jumped up and smacked his hands together with excitement.

"Then consider me on board and in charge of manning the grill." He shuffled towards the back door and his small back yard that was mostly filled with a picnic table, bench seats and a whole area dedicated to the fine art of grilling. This was the version of my dad I'd dreamed of, and wished for all my life.

It was better late than never, that's what I told myself every time. There was a time I didn't think Dad would ever put the bottle down, so I hadn't hoped for it, didn't wish for things to be different. But it had happened, and without any pushing from me, so I took every good moment we had together and I cherished it.

With Dad busy in the yard tinkering with the grill, I set my phone up on the little stand I bought for dad so he could listen to music or sports while he worked in the kitchen.

"Let's see if you're as good a teacher as you are a brooding bad boy," I told the thumbnail and then pressed play.

Antonio

✥

"You two are disgusting. Think you can stop pawing each other for at least a few minutes?" I shook my head at the twosome that was supposed to be my guests for today's video shoot.

Cal flashed a smile as he took his lips off my sister and shrugged. "You said this was for a romantic dinner, so we're setting the scene."

"The *scene* is about the food. All I need from you is some hand holding and loving smiles, not a porno re-enactment."

Teddy snickered. "I thought you were happy for us."

"I am, but that doesn't mean I want to see you suck face right in front of me. Or feed each other. Or lick each other's fingers. Have some restraint, yeah?" It was hard enough to watch my kid sister fall in love even though I knew it was going to happen eventually. I was happy it was a guy as good as Cal, but it was awkward as hell to see them all lovey-dovey together. "Now, do you think you two can act like adults and not horny teenagers for the next twenty minutes?"

"Twenty minutes," Teddy shouted, her big brown eyes wide with surprise. "That's a long video for you."

"I need twenty minutes so I can edit it down, which means no more kissing and no more groping. Act like you're in public and keep it PG. Okay?"

"Twenty *whole* minutes?" Cal whined but his eyes sparkled with mischief and I knew he was just screwing with me. "It'll be hard, but I think we can manage. Right babe?"

"Sure we can." Teddy flashed a wide smile that spelled trouble as she reached for the bottle of wine on the table. "We've got fancy wine so it must be a special occasion."

"The winery is sponsoring this video and they sent a case." The wine was decent, which was a good thing, because it made me feel like less of a sellout for recommending products before I tested them. The money was good and the exposure would help a lot, but that feeling lingered.

"Awesome, can we drink while you do your spiel?"

"As long as drinking doesn't make either of you frisky."

"I make no promises," Teddy teased.

"Then I can't promise you won't get a raw meatball to the head."

She gasped and narrowed her gaze. "You wouldn't."

I blinked and fixed my face into an innocent expression. "Food fights aren't romantic?"

"Jerk," she growled and pulled the cork on the bottle set on the table. "Now you have to *set* a new bottle."

I let that slide, because it was important to get this video under way before I had to make more bread to get the perfect image of a freshly baked, steaming hot loaf.

With lingering threat of flying meatballs, I managed to get all the footage I needed in thirty minutes. "Thanks guys. That's a wrap."

"Oh thank good," Teddy growled. "Now I can eat for real."

Cal laughed. "No one forced you to take those little bird bites."

Teddy glared at Cal in outrage. "You know his subscribers would rip me apart if I took a big ol' honking bite of pasta!" My sister, who gave no damns what anyone thought of her, was overly sensitive regarding the beliefs of online commenters.

"That's not true," I added with a smile. "There are plenty who want to see you naked. Some have offered a lot of money to see you topless or eating certain foods."

"Really?"

I nodded. "Really, and it's disturbing."

"Gross." Teddy gave a shudder and reached for the gnocchi. "I've definitely earned the right to eat without a camera in my face. Have a seat, Chef."

"You know, Teddy, ignoring the comments on my videos is an option." I felt responsible since I was the one who asked her to appear in my videos, but Teddy was honest to a fault, personable, and for the most part, she was a huge hit with my subscribers. "Everyone is a critic online."

She rolled her eyes and swallowed a mouthful of gnocchi with my homemade marinara. "Don't you think I wish I could stop reading them?"

"Or," Cal added, "you can stop focusing on the five negative comments and choose to be grossed out by the thousands of sexual comments. Those pervs come up with some creatives uses for food." He wiggled his eyebrows. "Ouch! What was that for?"

"I don't want to hear the kinky shit you do to my sister while I eat. Or ever," I added because I knew Cal would choose another time to bring it up just to piss me off."

"Damn." Cal snapped his finger and gave a pout that told me I was right about his intentions.

Thankfully, the food was so good that I managed to finish my plate before conversation started back up again. "Have you heard from Trishelle lately?"

I groaned at the mention of my ex-wife. "No, thank

god. Rosie is better off without her, and she's still embarrassed that I got full custody of her." Finding her laid out on the bathroom floor from an overdose had gone a long way to convince the judge that I was a better parent, but Trishelle had never forgiven me for it.

"I read in your comments section that she's filming a new reality show, so you should expect to hear from her sooner or later."

"Later is just fine by me." Her neglect had probably worsened Rosie's asthma and the longer she stayed out of our lives, the better.

"I know it's fine by you, Antonio, but what about Rosie? She's the girliest little girl the world has ever seen, and honestly, she needs more female influence than me." Teddy looked down at the green dress she'd worn for the date night video and sighed. "This isn't me. I wear jeans all the time, and I'm constantly covered in dirt. She needs to see examples of all types of women."

"You're fine," I insisted, in part because I didn't want to talk about my love life, or lack thereof, again. "Not all women wear frilly dresses and makeup all the time."

"I know that, dummy. But I was already a tomboy before Mom died, and being surrounded by males finished me off, but Rosie isn't like me."

"Finished you off? What's that supposed to mean?"

We all chipped in to help out after our mom died, doing the best we could to stay a family.

"It means that I had a lot of questions that Dad and Cenzo couldn't answer. Which was better, pads or tampons? How do tampons even work? The difference between eyeliner and mascara. Padded bras or underwire? It was confusing as hell, and I was too embarrassed to talk to anyone other than Hannah about it. Eventually it was easier just to be one of the guys when it was possible."

I blinked twice, surprised that her words hit me like the tip of a whip. "You never said a thing."

"Because it wasn't a big deal. To me. Rosie is a girly girl, and if that's who she is, I don't want her to stifle it just to fit in." Teddy's tone was soft and sympathetic, but I couldn't help the anger that filled me at her insinuation.

"You think I'm depriving Rosie."

"No. But think about what you want for Rosie in the future. You want her to have everything she wants, right?"

"Duh."

Teddy nodded. "What if that's a husband or wife and kids?"

"I would never deprive Rosie of that!"

"Not on purpose, no. But just because your ex-wife is a garbage person doesn't mean you want Rosie to grow up thinking relationships are bad and should be avoided at all costs. Do you?

"No." I wanted Rosie to have every little thing her heart desired, and I worked my ass off to make it possible.

"Then maybe do something about it. I'm not suggesting that you have to get into a relationship, get married or even get serious about a woman if that's not what you want. But maybe get some female friends, actual friends that you don't have sex with, so that she has more women in her life."

"She has you and she has Hannah. Hannah is girly."

Cal laughed. "Hannah wears dresses sure, but you do know she runs a DIY site, don't you?"

"Yeah, she makes crafts and stuff."

Teddy snorted a laugh. "The *and stuff* was a smoker last month, a tool carrier a few weeks ago, and this week she's planning on turning an old saw blade into a knife."

"Really? Cool. I had no idea."

Teddy growled and Cal laughed. "You're missing the point. Hannah is more like me in all ways but appearance. I said variety, Antonio."

I nodded and poured another glass of wine, feeling better about the footage I shot with every sip. "You've given me some things to think about, Teddy."

"I'm not criticizing you, Cal."

"I know, it's just something I hadn't really considered."

She smiled sympathetically. "Because you're not a motherless little girl, that's why I brought it up."

"Thanks." For the rest of the day, I thought about my sister's words and wondered where in the hell I could find female friends who I didn't want to sleep with and who wouldn't get ideas about picket fences and wedding dresses if I asked them to hang out.

Instantly an image of a wavy haired redhead appeared. Augusta wasn't all that impressed by me.

I could work with that.

Gus

✦✦✦

"Please don't tell me someone stole my car."

I just finished an unscheduled double shift because two ER nurses were down with the flu, and the last thing I needed was a stolen vehicle. My eyes were so heavy I knew I had just enough energy to get home myself safely. I was so exhausted I wasn't sure my legs would hold me up much longer.

And now my car was missing. "What's wrong, Gus?"

I turned at the sound of Cal's voice, sounding as tired as mine since we'd just finished ten hours in the ER together.

"My car is gone."

"Need a ride home? It's been a long night."

"No, if someone stole it I'd like to file a report quickly so hopefully the police find it before it's been stripped for parts." The thought was so daunting I sighed again. "But thanks for the offer. You should get home."

Cal hoisted his backpack over his shoulder and slowly surveyed the parking lot, moving a few yards in each direction. "Hey Gus?"

"Yeah," I sighed.

"Isn't this your car?" He pointed to my little white four-door with the dancing daisy sticker on the back. "Maybe you're more tired than you think."

Maybe, but as I drew closer to my car, my steps slowed. All the mud from the big puddle I'd driven through was gone. There was no splatter on the side doors or my windshield. "How strange."

"What?"

"Someone washed my car."

Cal laughed. "Can you ask the fairy to hook me up next?"

I shrugged and unlocked the door, and I was immediately hit with the scent of oranges. I bent down to look inside my car and gasped. The little baggie filled with trash was gone, the mats had been vacuumed and even the seats were free of crumbs and discarded napkins.

"Someone cleaned my car." I had no idea who would do such a thing. Not until I spotted the red and silver thermal bag sitting on the passenger seat, a note taped to it written in Dad's chicken scratch.

"You're not the only one who's good at taking care of those he loves. Love, Ollie."

Tears welled up in my eyes even as a small smile ghosted around the edges of my lips. This was such a difference from the man I'd grown up with, who couldn't be bothered with simple tasks like grocery shopping or paying the bills, leaving me to do it all. I cleaned the house, washed our clothes and even signed my own report cards and permission slips. I'd been mother and father to myself back then, and he'd been, well he was just drunk.

This little gesture, cleaning my car and feeding me, didn't make up for that, but I was happy to have my dad back.

The smells coming from the thermal bag taunted me on the short drive to my house, but by the time I made my way home, all I wanted was a hot shower and my bed, which I gave myself in short order. I fell into bed wearing nothing but my towel and I didn't wake up until my alarm sounded six hours later, refreshed and ready to enjoy what was left of my impromptu day off.

The first thing I did was head for the kitchen, opting for tea instead of coffee since it was well past noon, and I pulled the thermal bag from the oven, smiling when I found the wrapped food still warm. Dad had gone above and beyond with his gesture by cleaning my car and leaving me food, but the homemade touch was sweet. I dug into the breakfast tacos and waffle fries with maple butter with more energy than a girl desperately trying to drop fifteen pounds should. But it was so good.

I reached for my phone and dialed Dad but the call went straight to voicemail. "Hey Dad, I just wanted to thank you for taking care of my car and me. Breakfast is yummy." I ended the call with a smile, happy that I didn't automatically start calling hospitals and police stations in search of my father. Those days were gone, and it was more likely he was off fishing or enjoying the many things on offer at Jackson's Ridge Community Center.

Since Dad was busy, I got dressed and went to Better Baked where my friend Megan worked, performing magic with butter, sugar and flour. I found her smiling at a pair of elderly flirts from her spot behind the counter, smiling like the old timers had a chance with the happily married woman.

"The women of this town better watch out for those silver tongues."

The old men blushed, took their coffee and pastries and took up on the patio where they could watch the world go by. Megan looked at them wistfully and I wondered what that was about.

"Thinking of trading in Casey for one of the silver foxes?"

Megan blinked and then laughed. "No way, I've got the face and hands of McDreamy with the body of McSteamy rolled into one. What more could a girl ask for?"

"What, indeed?" We shared a laugh and I ordered my favorite chocolate and pecan croissants. "Do you have time to catch up? It feels like ages since we've had a chance to chat."

Megan nodded. "Grab a seat and I'll bring out some goodies for us." I barely had a chance to get settled before Megan sat down with two large coffees, croissants and some new creation she was working on. "Okay, let's chat. How's life at the hospital?"

I laughed. "Your husband is the neurosurgeon, and you still want to engage in more hospital talk? No wonder he's so stupidly smitten with you after all these years."

Megan grinned. "Look at you, sounding like you've lived here for your whole life." She rolled her eyes. "Casey gets thirty minutes to bitch and moan about work before we focus on other things. Same for me."

"How very mature of you both."

She shrugged. "It works. What about you, are you seeing anyone?"

"You mean have I broken my six month dry spell? No and nope, I have not and I'm fine with that." Well, *fine* was an oversimplification of the facts, but small town living made dating difficult. You had to be careful about burning bridges you might need later while also avoiding awkwardness at potluck dinners, festivals and all the other town-wide events that seemed to take place every week.

"You're fine with not getting laid for six months? I'm calling bullshit, Gus."

"I'm not getting laid in the traditional sense, but my needs are being met. Besides, it's not like men are banging down my door to take out the plump kiddie nurse." That's what they all saw and I knew it. I was learning to love my curves, but it was a process. I was learning to accept who I was, and that meant accepting the truth, no matter how bitter it tasted.

Megan took a long sip of her coffee, her green eyes blazing a hole right through me. She studied me carefully before she spoke. "That's crap, and I really hope you know that Gus because you're gorgeous. I mean, I'd kill to have the hourglass curves you have, and those boobs, my goodness they're a work of art even if you do try to hide them at every opportunity. Your sexy waves and almond shaped green eyes make you look like a mermaid. You are beautiful, and I'm sure plenty of men in town think so."

I blinked, shocked at her words. I mean, I don't think I'm ugly, but I'm very realistic about what I look like, and it wasn't what Megan described. "That's what friends are supposed to say, but if you really mean it you can leave Casey and date me since I'm so gorgeous and all."

Megan laughed and leaned over to take in the green dress that fell just past my knees. "You can totally be my side chick, because I love Casey too much to leave him."

I sighed and fake pouted. "See, even you only want me as your dirty little secret."

Megan laughed and shook her head. "I think your mirrors are broken honey, but we'll talk more about that when we have tacos and tequila. What are you up to the rest of the day?"

"Good question. After eating two croissants and that lemon bar, I guess my first stop will be the gym. Then I'll see if I can catch up with Dad." I told her about what he did and the note. "Those waffle fries were to die for!"

Megan's face lit up with a wide smile. "That's great, Gus. I'm so happy to hear the move is working out for you both."

"I wasn't sure having him move here would work out, but he really is sober and doing well. I love spending time with him."

"Awesome," she popped the miniature lemon white chocolate bar in her mouth. "Now let's talk about those waffle fries and getting you laid."

"I can help on both counts," a deep voice said, and I knew that voice well. It had starred in too many of my fantasies lately, not to mention guided me through dozens of new recipes.

My nipples beaded into tight little buds and my belly clenched. I swallowed hard before looking up at Antonio. Two words came to mind, *yes, please*.

Antonio

I shouldn't have been eavesdropping. I knew that from the moment I heard Augusta's honeyed voice, but I just couldn't' help myself.

The men in this town must be idiots to let this gorgeous woman with such a hot body spend her nights alone, and even worse, thinking that those curves weren't appreciated. Six months? That was unreal. It was a goddamn travesty is what it was. Hearing that, or maybe it was the pragmatic way she said the words, forced the words from my mouth.

Megan laughed as I knew she would, because the pretty baker appreciated a good flirting session.

Augusta looked up at me with wide green eyes, darkened with a hint of lust. I watched her pulse flutter in her neck, took stock of her glazed over eyes and slightly open mouth. Yeah, she wanted me, even if she didn't want to. "Seriously?"

I nodded. "Yeah. Six months is a long time, Augusta."

"No kidding," she agreed with a half amused grunt of laughter.

"No woman should have to go without an orgasm for so long."

One reddish gold brow arched. "Who said I've been without an orgasm?"

Now *that* question instantly brought forth images of her splayed out naked on her back, legs spread wide as she pleasured herself. Did she watch porn? Did she use her attraction to me as inspiration?

"I'm much better than batteries," I assured her and ignored the press of my cock to my zipper.

"Cockier, that's for sure."

I shrugged because Augusta wasn't wrong, I was a cocky son of a bitch. "In more ways than one, sweetheart." I winked and she gifted me with another of those eyerolls I couldn't get enough of. Probably because I knew it was a defence mechanism.

"So you're hung, you've got wicked staying power and you're gorgeous? I wonder why the women in town aren't banging down your door." She tapped her chin like she was really giving it some thought as her gaze slid to my crotch and the growing bulge I was powerless to hide.

The fact that she was attracted me but didn't seem to like me very much was a strange twist that I couldn't resist. "Who said they aren't?" They were, in droves truthfully. But I was already burned once by a woman who chose drugs over her family, and I wasn't putting myself in that position again. No way. No how. No thanks.

"Right." She drew the word out for several long seconds as her green eyes filled with heat once again. For a second I thought maybe she would take me up on my offer, but then the stubborn woman changed the subject. "I made your char Siu for my dad the other day. It was a big hit. Be cocky about that."

Holy shit, those words were even hotter than the green dress that showed off miles of cleavage that had my mouth watering to taste her. "You subscribe to my channel?"

"Yeah. Turns out you're a pretty good teacher, and I'm expanding my culinary horizons thanks to you." She was sincere, and now I really wanted her, which meant I would have her. In time.

I grabbed a chair from the table beside where Augusta and Megan sat, turning it backwards to hide the effect sparring with the pretty nurse was having on me. "You have me right here in town and you learn from the internet? I'm hurt."

Augusta laughed, and it was a pretty sound, husky

and feminine. "I can unsubscribe if you want. I'm sure there are other tattooed chefs I can learn from when my schedule allows it."

"No need to be hasty," I assured her because subscribers helped me pay the bills. "But I could give you a few lessons if you'd like."

She arched a brow and folded her arms, skepticism written all over her face. "Is that a euphemism, or is it a genuine offer?"

It was my turn to laugh. "Can't it be both?"

"It could," she conceded, "but I know guys like you, all talk with a disappointing show. Maybe there's some assistant behind the camera doing all the hard work."

"You can ask Ollie. Who do you think made that breakfast you were drooling over?"

"You?"

I nodded, and I couldn't help my satisfied smile. "Yeah. I melted the butter with the maple syrup and let it firm up again, that's why it's so smooth and spreadable."

Augusta licked her lips and once again, those emerald eyes darkened to a deep forest green. She turned her gaze away from me and faced Megan, who offered up an encouraging, wide-eyed smile.

"Fine," she turned back to me with a deliberately bored expression. "I accept the offer of cooking lessons, but I *will* resist your other offer."

"You can try, Augusta, but we'll see, won't we?" I could already see her riding my cock, I could taste her sweet juices, those plump tits as her red hair spread across my pillow. Down her shoulders. Our bodies slick with sweat.

"Yeah, we will," she insisted, her chin notched high in the air, defiant as hell.

"I can't wait to get started." That much was the truth. I had plenty of women ask for cooking lessons, but every single time was a euphemism for other things. "Come by tonight at six for the first lesson."

She frowned. "Who said I'm free tonight?"

"Cal. Said you were pulled into a double shift with him in the ER. He's off so you are too. Right?"

She grinned. "Stalker, much?"

"Nope, not much. Just a little."

Megan giggled and stood as she fanned her face. "All right you two, I'm off before you set the whole place on fire. Talk to you later, Gus."

"We didn't finish our conversation," she insisted to Megan's retreating back.

I laughed at how worried she looked about being left alone with me, but really, it boosted my confidence. "Six o'clock. Don't be late. And please, keep the dress on, I have aprons to protect your clothes." The shocked expression on her face, the slight parting of her plump lips, was so damn satisfying that I walked out of Better Baked without my weekly éclair fix.

I would just have to make some myself when I got home and have Augusta test them out for me later. Oh yeah, I liked that plan better.

A hell of a lot better.

Gus

t five minutes to six o'clock, I stood on Antonio's doorstep and rang the door bell, the green dress I had on earlier was laying on my bed in favor of a pair of jeans and a plain white t-shirt. I was sure Antonio was just messing with me and had no designs to take me to dinner or to bed, but just to be safe I decided to show up without the dress.

The front door opened and Antonio stood there in the same black t-shirt and gray jeans he had on earlier, a little bit of flour stained the t-shirt and his feet were bare. He shoved one hand in his pocket and smiled as he looked me up and down.

"I knew you would change."

I shrugged. "Then you're not disappointed."

"The hell I'm not. I was looking forward to peeking

down your cleavage whenever I could. Now I'll settle for staring at that pink lace bra under your t-shirt."

Of course he noticed. It was foolish to think he wouldn't. I rolled my eyes to try and stop the smile that threatened at his words. "Are you gonna invite me in, or are we cooking outside?" Cooking outdoors might have been better than being squeezed into a tight space with this larger than life man.

Antonio stepped back, a small step that forced me to brush against him as I entered his home. "Welcome to Casa Ricci."

His words came from right beside my ear, and I closed my eyes to ward off the temptation to lean into him. I didn't open them until his warmth faded and there was distance between us. Antonio's place was unexpected. There was plush carpeting and comfortable furniture in the living room, a giant plastic bin full of toys and a flat screen TV mounted on the wall. Well, I guess the presence of the toys was not really surprising.

"I'm surprised at how homey your place is."

His laugh was loud and booming, but most of all good-natured. "Were you expecting calendars with naked women? A pool table in the living room and a keg in the corner?"

"No." I rolled my eyes and took my time as I looked at all the photos on the wall of him and Rosie, him and his brothers and sister, and of course Cal. It was all family. "I expected leather furniture, hard wood floors and a TV so large it could be viewed from space." I shook my head and motioned around the room. "There's more Rosie here than you, at least what I know of you anyway." Which was, admittedly, not much, so what would I know?

Antonio folded his arms, either to intimidate me or arouse me, I didn't know so I diverted my gaze from his tattooed biceps back to the family photos. "Yeah? And what is it you think you know about me Augusta?" There was a challenge in is deep brown eyes and it made me curious what he thought I would say.

I held up a hand, speaking directly to Antonio without looking at him, and ticked off what I knew with a finger. "Pro chef who was poised to become the next big thing. Loving father. Good teacher. Confirmed bachelor. Oh, and cocky as hell."

Antonio stared at me oddly, and I dropped my hand as the odd look turned to surprise.

"Did I miss something? A hidden talent I should know about?" I didn't listen to gossip in town unless it was unavoidable, and even then I didn't assume that it was all facts. I just listened.

"I have many hidden talents, and you'll know about them. Soon." The man just couldn't help himself, his flirt button was always on. I didn't think he had an off button.

"Oh boy."

He shrugged. "Most people bring up my ex-wife."

"Ex-wife? I wasn't aware you were ever married."

Antonio's tension faded and his shoulders relaxed. "I was. Now, I'm not."

"Why do people bring her up?"

"You really don't know?"

I shook my head. "My interest in you outside the hospital is your videos, Antonio."

And just like that, his expression was back to sexy. "Ready for lesson number one?"

I nodded eagerly, because if we were talking food, we weren't flirting. And if we weren't flirting, then maybe I could pretend he didn't smell like heaven and sex all rolled into one. I could pretend being this close to him didn't completely overwhelm my senses.

"As ready as I'll ever be."

"Good." He paused for a long minute, raked a hand through his hair, and turned to grab a few things from a cabinet behind him. "You seem so capable at all times, Augusta. Why are you just learning to cook now?"

I tried to shrug off the question, but before I knew it, real details flew from my mouth. "As a kid I took care of myself most of the time and my culinary education was focused on quick and easy, or just plain convenient. Bologna sandwiches. Grilled cheese. Canned ravioli and spaghetti. Frozen dinners. You know, the fancy stuff."

His lips tugged into a lopsided grin. "I'm familiar with them."

"Yeah well, now I'm trying to eat healthier, and I'm told that starts with whole foods, which means I need to know what to do with 'em." I shook my head and mentally checked myself for sharing so much with Antonio. "What's lesson number one?"

"Salad dressing." He laughed at the pout I sent him. "You eat salad all the time," he growled at me. "You women and your diets, I'll never understand it."

"Because you're fit and you've probably always been in excellent shape." Men never understood, and I stopped explaining years ago.

"Excellent shape, huh?" His dark brows rose in surprise, lips twisted into an amused grin.

"Back to the salad dressing, Romeo."

His deep chuckle echoed in the quiet kitchen. "The reason you don't like salad is because you can't eat enough store bought dressing without overloading on calories. I'm going to blow your mind with this basic vinaigrette."

I ignored the zing of pleasure that tore through me and lifted my chin high in the air. "Challenge accepted."

"Good. Now, your basic vinaigrette only requires two things, oil and acid, but if you want you can reduce or eliminate the oil altogether." While he spoke, Antonio's hands moved gracefully like a pianist, adding a pinch of this and a dash of that to the small glass bowl. "You could also use mustard or miso paste in place of the oil for a thick and flavorful vinaigrette that won't break the calorie bank." He flashed a smile while he whisked like crazy, until the mixture was thick and frothy. "Now it's your turn."

I looked at the ingredients he set out into three categories, oil, acid and seasoning, and grabbed what I needed. "What about you, why did you become a chef?"

"Feeding five kids plus Dad was a big task, and we used to take turns doing it with a range of outcomes, from burnt, to call the fire department. My food was always the best, so Cenzo redid the chore list so that my only responsibility was cooking. Well, and grocery shopping, except during football season."

I let out a grunt while I whisked. "Of course you played football. Quarterback?"

"Nah, that was Cal. I played wide receiver." Antonio let out another loud laugh at the blank look on my face. "Not a football fan?"

"Nope. How'd I do?"

He examined the bowl first and then stuck a finger in to scoop some up, and sweet lord the way he licked his finger sent my poor libido into overdrive. "Delicious."

"Cool. I'm sure I can remember oil, acid and seasonings."

"If you forget, I'm just a phone call away." He smiled as if he knew I wanted to say something smart ass back to him and continued on. "Next is the ulti-mate salad dressing. Ranch." He gave me a recipe and tips to make my second favorite dressing at home. "A lot healthier than the store bought stuff, just from the lack of added preservatives alone. Much cheaper too."

I didn't know how he knew to avoid all the trigger words, like calorie friendly and less sugar, but it was a relief. Maybe I'll actually lose those final fifteen from nursing school without all the perceived judgement from outside sources. "You're helping me to understand a ton Antonio, I might have to start liking you."

He shook his head and leaned across the counter that separated us. "You already like me, Augusta. You just don't want to."

I could have denied it, but Antonio Ricci was more than just a pretty face, in fact he was pretty damn astute, so I shrugged. "True. But you're trouble, and I'm not in the market for trouble right now. It's nothing personal," I added, even though you couldn't really say something like that to someone without it being personal.

"Trouble?" His tone was surprised, as if no one had ever told him he was the walking talking definition of the word.

I nodded and whipped up a tahini and ginger dressing with a proud smile as I held it out to him. "Yeah, the kind of trouble that usually ends with too much chocolate ice cream and red wine. Heartbreak."

"I don't break hearts," he insisted with a sincerity that was as funny as it was sad.

"Of course you do, even if you don't mean to." That was the problem with men like Antonio, they were nice guys, likable men who were charming and sexy and even sweet at times, so much so that you forgot that you're not supposed to fall for them. Then you do, and it's too late to turn back. "You clearly don't trust women, and I'm not in the market for a casual fling."

"What's wrong with having a casual fling?"

"Nothing at all. I've had a few in my life, enough to know that I can't do casual. I can't just have sex with someone when it doesn't mean anything." I tried, three times to be exact, and each time I found myself crying into a bucket of ice cream and wetting my throat with copious amounts of wine.

Antonio rounded the counter between us and took the bowl from my hands before he gripped my shoulders and turned me so we faced each other. His brown eyes were dark and intense. "There's no such thing as meaningless sex. The meaning is pleasure, Augusta. Yours. Mine. Our collective pleasure. That's the point. At least for me, it is."

I let out a shaky breath at his words and the hunger

49

in his voice, and I had to take a step back to get a moment of relief. "I can't Antonio."

"Not yet, but you will." It was an ominous prediction that felt more like a promise.

And what was worse? I had a feeling he was right.

Antonio

❧✿❧

"I like to swing high, Daddy. Really, really high!"

Rosie bounced along the sidewalk beside me, a bright smile on her face from an hour spent at the park after a morning of arts and crafts at the community center. As much as everyone told me I needed to give my little girl some freedom, I was determined to get her involved in as many relaxing activities as possible. Like arts and crafts. And sewing. And even learning how to do makeup.

That's how desperate I was.

"I noticed. You're the reason my muscles stay so big, all that pushing." I flexed and made funny faces, letting her giggles wash over me.

"I feel like I'm flying!"

Yeah, she was a miniature version of me, the same daredevil spirit that had caused many broken arms, bruised ribs and more than one broken nose. "I'm glad you had a good time at the park."

"Next time you should swing too."

"But then you wouldn't get to go so high." Her little legs weren't strong enough to get the height she required to laugh and squeal with delight.

"Okay," she sighed, somewhat disappointed. I heard a gasp and prepared to freak out and rush her to the ER when she started to scream. "Mr. Ollie! Mr. Ollie! Over here!"

Oliver Thompson. Augusta's father had become one of Rosie's favorite people in town. For some reason, his grumpy disposition amused my daughter and she was always excited to see him. With a green and white cooler in one hand and a fishing pole in the other, he lifted the fishing pole in greeting.

"Princess Rosie. How are you today?"

"I'm good. I made a crown for one of my dollies and a bracelet for Aunty Teddy. Oh, and I made something for you too," she shouted and then leaned in with a conspiratorial grin. "It's a surprise."

"Sounds like you've had a busy day. I thought all you royals lived a life of leisure?"

She giggled. "What's that?"

"It means you don't do anything all day, just look pretty and eat lots of good food."

Rosie let out another laugh. "I did lots today. How are you?"

I couldn't help but smile at her manners. She often forgot, and I didn't really get on her because she was still a little girl, but when she remembered it made me feel like I wasn't screwing everything up.

Ollie sighed. "Good, good. Had a fine day at the fishing hole." He held up the cooler with a satisfied smile. "How would you two like to attend an old-fashioned fish fry?"

"What's that?" Rosie's gaze bounced between me and Ollie, waiting for an explanation.

"It's just what it sounds like, little girl. We get together and fry up some fish, and some other things that go with fish. We talk and we laugh and sometimes we dance."

"I love dancing!" She turned to me with a devilish grin. "Can we Daddy?"

"I love a good fish fry as much as the next guy, and cooking happens to be my specialty."

Ollie grunted. "Nothing too fancy, Antonio. It's a fish fry, not a fish ball."

Rosie giggled and shook her head, putting a small smile on Ollie's face.

"Let's stop at my place for a few things first, and then me and Rosie will walk back with you." Ollie nodded and fell into step beside me, nodding patiently as Rosie regaled him with every detail of her day.

She didn't even stop when we arrived home. "I'm gonna get your surprise Mr. Ollie, be back real soon!"

By the time I returned with a bag of things to contribute to the fish fry, Ollie wore a gentle smile as he watched Rosie talk to the fish inside the cooler. "She made me a lure. It's glittery as hell and brighter than the sun, but it's nice. Really nice." The old man seemed touched by the gesture, and I wondered if his relationship with Rosie was his way of making things right with the world.

Inside Ollie's brown and white ranch house, he set down his hook and took the cooler to the mudroom, Rosie on his heels. "Whatcha gonna do, Mr. Ollie?"

His footsteps stopped inside the mudroom and he turned to her. "This part isn't meant for princesses, sorry little girl."

"Okay." And just like that she turned to me and climbed into a chair where she busied herself with the important work of coloring.

Ollie split the fish between us with a grunt and made his way to the grill in the backyard, where he seemed happiest. When I joined him a few minutes later with corn and potatoes for the grill, I noticed it was the first time I'd seen him wear anything but a scowl.

"You've got a good stash of vegetables, Ollie."

He half-grunted, half-laughed. "My stubborn daughter keeps buying the damn things, forcing me to eat them or have her waste her money on me." He shook his head as he made room for the vegetables on the grill. "It's a damn trap, I tell yah."

"Oh the horror of having someone care about your well-being." My sarcasm was heavy and Ollie sent me a narrow eyed glare.

"Throwing my words back at me? That's low, Chef. Really low." We burst out laughing, knowing that Ollie had told me the same thing on multiple occasions when I complained about how overly helpful my siblings had been since I returned to Jackson's Ridge.

"What's so funny?" Augusta's voice startled me, and judging by the look on his face, Ollie too. Rosie however was perched on her hip, arms casually wrapped around her neck.

"Nothing," we answered at the same time and then burst out laughing once again.

Augusta's green eyes narrowed before her lips curled into a grin. "Oh, that's not suspicious. Not at all." She rolled her eyes and took in the food on the grill, the tongs in my hands and Ollie's. "I just stopped by to say hi, Dad, but I see you're busy, so I'll give you a call tomorrow."

"No, stay! Please," Rosie pleaded.

"You'll stay," Ollie insisted in a tone that brooked no argument.

Augusta's reddish gold brows dipped low. "Are you sure? I don't want to intrude." I could see curiosity burning in her eyes at the scene before her, but my connection to her father wasn't my business to tell.

"Course I'm sure," Ollie grunted. "You can judge who makes a better fish filet."

I laughed at her father's indirect challenge. "There's no contest, obviously mine is better."

"Don't be so sure, boy. I know all your tricks, Mr. TV Personality." He chuckled at his sometimes nickname for me.

"I'm not on TV," I reminded him. "Or is your memory not what it used to be?"

Ollie let out a loud bark of laughter. "You're in my house. Augusta set up my whole TV so it's all internet based, including your channel." He flashed a proud smile at Augusta, who stared back in wide-eyed shock. "Pretty cool, ain't it?"

I watched the curious play of emotions on Augusta's face before she realized she had my full attention and turned to me. I winked, and Augusta rolled her eyes. "It was nothing, Dad. Really."

"Sure was something to me. Got way more stuff to watch than we had in my day."

"Who knew you had so many talents, Augusta? Maybe you can help with mine?"

"Maybe," she shrugged. "But I'm sure one of your YouTube friends could help."

I laughed because I wouldn't let her out of this little corner so easily. "Why would I ask them when I have you right here?"

Augusta wasn't happy that I pushed, and she took advantage of Rosie's need for freedom to collect herself. She stood and put her hands on her ample hips. "Fine. When I have time I'll come around and walk you through it."

Just the acquiescence I needed. "We could do it now. It won't take long to fry the fish, and those potatoes will need some time on the grill."

"Yeah!" Ollie's shout visibly startled Rosie and Augusta. "That's perfect. Princess Rosie can prove she doesn't live a life of leisure by being my chef assistant."

"Sous chef," I offered with a grin.

"Yeah, that's it, you can be my sous chef."

"'Kay!" Rosie was eager to please, more so when she felt like she was being helpful. It was normal the child psychologist said, but I had a feeling it had something to do with the time she spent with Trishelle.

"Oh, fine. Come on, then." Augusta drove, even though my house was only three blocks away, probably hoping to speed things along or avoid three blocks worth of conversation.

"You didn't have to do this," I told her, my eyes glued to her ass, high in the air while she bent over to inspect my modem.

Holy hell when she turned a glare over her shoulder at me, I could picture her in that same position, only naked and telling me how she wanted to be pleased.

"Don't give me that crap after you painted me into a corner just to get me here."

She was right, of course. "I just asked. You said yes because you secretly wanted to help me out."

She snorted and shook her head as she stood. "Whatever you need to tell yourself, Ricci." Augusta kept her green eyes on the television, typing in a series of letters and numbers with the remote, testing and retesting the internet connection. "There. All done. YouTube. Netflix. Roku. Whatever your thing is, there it is." She pointed to the screen with a small but satisfied grin.

"Thanks."

"No problem." She folded her arms, the move pushing her tits up and right into my line of sight. "When did you and my dad become friends?"

"A few months ago," I shrugged. I answered her question without giving her the answer she really wanted.

"How did you meet him."

"At the community center." The truth, but not the whole truth.

She rolled her eyes again, but this time a small smile curved her lips into a half circle. "He loves that place."

"It's a good place." Ollie helped people there, and in the process helped himself, but for some reason he didn't want Augusta to know.

"I guess."

"I know," I told her as I stepped closer to her. The air between us crackled with electricity, making the hairs on my arms stand up.

"Antonio," she whispered and put a hand to my chest, intending to give me a shove, but that never happened. "Don't."

"Don't what, Augusta? Don't touch you?" The words came out soft and I took a lock of her hair between my thumb and forefinger, and followed the crinkle of her wave all the way down to the end. "Don't kiss you? Because I want to."

"Right. Okay. Ready to go?" Augusta took a step back, escape written all over her pretty face, but my hands went to her hips.

"No, I'm not ready. Not yet." I let my fingers sweep up her hips until her head was cradled in my hand, and then I brought my lips to her sweet mouth, drinking in the taste of her. My tongue swept across her lips, back and forth along the seam until she opened up and invited me in with a gasp.

She softened and leaned into the kiss, the delicious weight of her body sinking against mine had my cock standing at attention. Her soft tits pressed against my chest, the points of her nipples sharp and hard. She gasped and I deepened the kiss, savoring the taste of her, the way her tongue danced with mine.

When Augusta's fingers tangled in my hair, I sent a prayer up to my busy schedule that I hadn't gone in for the trim I needed, and pressed my hand into the center of her back, keeping those curves pressed tightly against me. The kiss went on and on, for long minutes. My body grew hotter by the second and I was eager to take Augusta upstairs and strip her down.

Too soon though, she pulled back with glazed over green eyes and kiss slicked lips. "That was...nice. Very nice. But we shouldn't do it again."

Nice? "It was a hell of a lot better than nice," I growled at her and focused my eyes on her chest. "Your nipples think so, anyway."

Augusta shook her head, red waves falling around her shoulders. "Antonio, this was a mistake."

"It wasn't. I know it and you do too. But sure Augusta, we can go."

Her shoulders fell as the tension released and she nodded. "Good." She turned on her heels and marched towards the front door.

"But it will happen again. You can be damn sure of that."

Her feet froze as if they were glued to the floor and she let out a shaky breath, a sound that went straight to my cock. "Antonio," she groaned.

I took three big steps and I was right behind her, bending down to whisper in her ear. "The next time you say my name like that, you'll be naked and my mouth will be all over you, pulling those sounds from your sweet mouth."

She gasped again and shook her head, probably to clear the haze of lust. "Antonio," she whispered again, the word husky this time.

I clasped her hand with mine and smiled. "Come on, we've got a fish try to get to, and suddenly I'm hungry as hell."

She looked into my eyes and let out a strangled groan before taking her hand back and slipping behind the steering wheel.

Game on, sweetheart.

Gus

❦

"I had fun, Nurse Gus. And I like your daddy a lot." Rosie wore the kind of all encompassing smile that only a well loved kid could as she launched herself at me. "His fish was better too," she whispered with a mischievous expression.

I accepted the love contained within her hug and squeezed her back. "Your secret is safe with me, Princess." Antonio's fish was by far the better of the two, crispy and full of flavor, but Rosie preferred her fish without the crunch. "I had a good time too. Thanks for letting me crash your party."

She pulled back with a grin and a wave for me and Dad. "Have a good night."

Antonio held his hand out for Rosie without taking his brown eyes off me. She slid her hand into his and he winked at me wordlessly. They pair walked down the street with the moon illuminating their retreating figures.

I closed the door and leaned against it with a sigh once the Ricci family was gone. Out of sight. I was happy to see that Dad was making friends and connections in town, but fighting my attraction to Antonio, especially after that kiss that set me on fire, was becoming a full-time job.

"What's going on with you and Antonio?" Dad's gravelly voice ended my moment of peace and I opened my eyes to see his smiling face a couple feet from my own.

"Nothing is going on," I answered a little too quickly. Dad might be getting up in age, but his eagle eyes didn't miss much. "He's got some kind of passing interest in me, probably out of boredom or proximity, but it won't last." In my experience, men's interest never lasted long. Usually they were gone the moment after they got what they wanted, or when it became clear they wouldn't get what they wanted from me.

"Why not?" Dad's wild brows dipped into a frown as if he really didn't get it, which only made me love him more. "What man wouldn't want a lovely, accomplished woman who's also good with kids? An idiot, that's who."

I took a step forward and wrapped my arms around my father and hugged him tight before I smacked a big kiss to his wrinkled cheek. "Thank you for saying that, but I think you might be a bit biased."

"Not at all, girl. I just call things how I see 'em." He winked with a wide eyed smile and I couldn't help but hug him again.

"Love you, Dad."

He sighed and reluctantly accepted the love I gave so freely. "Love you too, Augusta. Not sure I deserve it, but I sure am glad you asked me to move here. It's like a real community, one neither of us ever had before, and I'm finding that I like it. So, thank you."

"You're welcome, Dad. I'm happy you're here too."

He smiled and pulled me into the kitchen where we double teamed the dishes. "You could do a lot worse than Antonio, you know."

I laughed at his newfound interest in my nonexistent love life. "He's a heartbreaker dad, a man who isn't looking for love when that's all I've ever wanted." I had a string of broken relationships in my past that started with me wanting too much, and ended with him not wanting me enough to give it to me. A lifetime being deprived of that love had given me what some might call unrealistic relationship expectations, which mostly ended with me being disappointed every single time. Hence the six month break from dating. From men.

"That's bull, honey. I'm sorry, but it's true. All men are heartbreakers until they find that one woman who makes them want to change their ways."

And that was another relationship pitfall I tried to avoid. "I'm not interested in changing anyone, Dad." People didn't change for the most part, and trying wasn't just looking for heartache, it was begging for it.

Dad sighed as he handed me the last dish and turned to face me. "You don't have to change anyone, if a man loves you enough he will want to be worthy of yah. That's where the change comes in."

A nice thought, and I'd seen it firsthand with Cal and Teddy, but I wasn't one of those women who inspired that kind of fire in men. I wasn't a woman that a man wanted to change for, they expected me to accept them as they were, which I expected in return.

"Oh, my god." And suddenly it all made a lot of sense.

As the chubby girl, the girl with a few too many curves, all I wanted was a man to love me for me, not try to change me. But that meant I attracted men who didn't want to change either, who were happy to be with the plump chick as long as she didn't ask too much of them.

"What's going on in that pretty head of yours?" Dad's gravelly question pulled me from the depths of realization.

"I just realized my part in my failed relationships." And I vowed, then and there, to avoid making that mistake again. "Antonio won't change for me and I won't ask him to, so just drop it. Please?"

Dad held his hands up, red and still covered in suds, and sighed. "Fine, but let me just speak my peace and I'll be done with it."

"Go ahead."

"I know chemistry when I see it, and you and Antonio have it in spades. He might be a little rough around the edges but this thing between you might be worth exploring, no matter what you think you know about him. Okay, I'm done."

"You're just rooting for Antonio because you want gourmet food every night of the week." Of course, that wasn't entirely true. He and Antonio seemed to understand one another, which made me wonder what else they had in common that I didn't know about.

"I wouldn't say no to his cookin', but that's not the reason. Hell, in this town all I'd have to do is stand on the sidewalk and say I'm hungry and ten people will pop out the woodwork with ten different casseroles." He laughed and shook his head and I knew what he was feeling. It never failed to surprise me just how much the people of Jackson's Ridge were willing to step in and help out.

"Maybe I ought to stand out on the street and say that my dad is in search of female company, see who comes out of the woodwork for a handsome old man with a full head of hair and his own teeth."

He threw his head back and laughed. "You wouldn't do that to your old man, would you?"

I shrugged. "I might. Depends on how devious I'm feeling."

"Do that and I'll toss all the veggies from the fridge and replace 'em with soda and cheese puffs."

I laughed and shook my head. "Totally worth it to see you running away from a bunch of single seniors." The more I pictured his long, lanky body hurrying away from the widows and divorcees looking to start over, the harder I laughed.

"It ain't funny, girl."

His insistence only made me laugh harder until I was doubled over in the kitchen, tears running down my cheeks.

"Damn stubborn girl," he growled. "Lucky I love you."

In that moment, I felt incredibly lucky.

Antonio

✾

s much as I loved having a job that allowed me to spend as much time with Rosie as possible, I also appreciated that the community center offered dozens of classes and activities for kids under the age of ten. This allowed me to finish my production schedule for the next month. Planning wasn't just a necessity for my business, but also my life as a single dad. Planning allowed me to order hard to find ingredients and sign Rosie up for ballet when I had a shoot schedule that might trigger her asthma.

With just two more days to schedule out, I felt great about the progress I'd made this morning. There never seemed to be enough hours in the day, but I enjoyed the independence that being my own boss gave me. I didn't have to answer to anyone, which I loved, and my schedule was always my own. Some days I still longed for the chaos of a professional kitchen, but those days happened less and less often.

The phone buzzed on the kitchen table just as I slotted in the last shoot for the next thirty days and I sat back with a sigh. It was probably Travis or Cenzo, calling to see if I had any leftovers they could poach. "Antonio Ricci," I practically barked into the phone, because, as Teddy loved to tell me, my phone manners were atrocious.

"Antonio, it's Magda with some very good news for you. Are you sitting down?" My manager was a drama queen for sure, but she listened when I told her what I wanted and she only brought up shit I didn't want to do when the money was too good to pass up.

"Yeah, I'm sitting."

"Great. I've booked you an appearance on a cooking competition show, and the best part? You'll be there as a judge and not a lowly competitor, thanks to your bestselling cookbook and that award last month for being a top rated YT'er." Magda was giddier than I was over the accolades. As long as it meant I could keep supporting my family, I didn't give a damn.

"Sounds good, but when and how long?" I learned early on to get all the details before showing my cards.

"It's just one full day of shooting, the day after tomorrow, but it's in New York. Flight and hotel are paid for though." Magda's tone was hesitant, as if she thought I might reject the offer to appear on a national television show.

New York for twenty four hours. It wasn't ideal, but it was manageable. "All right Magda, I'm in."

"Excellent! Great! I'll let the producer know, and Antonio be sure to play up your bad boy image. Show off those gorgeous tattoos and maybe throw a leather jacket into the luggage. You know the drill."

I nodded because I did know the drill. The press, my manger and publicist all thought it was an image, but the truth was it was just me. The tattoos were another way to express my art, and the dark wardrobe was because I hated shopping and one of my girlfriends once told me that dark colors complimented my olive skin. It was an easy ask to fulfill, so I didn't bitch about it.

"I need to make arrangements for Rosie,so just send the travel details to my personal email."

"Done. I'll meet you in the hotel lobby at eight and take you to the studio. Laters."

"Perfect." As soon as the call ended, I dialed my sister first. "Can you watch Rosie for me? I need to go to New York for a day."

She sighed and my heart sank. "I wish I could say yeah, but we just started a renovation on a three-story Victorian that will appear in a national magazine which means all hands on deck to make the deadline."

"Damn, that's incredible. Good luck."

"Thanks," she laughed. "Travis is out too, so you might as well skip straight to Cenzo."

That's exactly what I did. "Vincenzo, my favorite brother. How's life treating you?"

He chuckled in amusement. "What do you need Antonio?"

"It's not me, it's for Rosie. She needs a babysitter while I head to the east coast for a shoot. Can you do it?"

"Only if you're all right with the princess spending the day at the office with me. That Victorian job means I'll be manning phones all day."

That was out of the question. "With all the debris and dust in the air, that's just asking for trouble."

"Sorry."

"No problem. Talk later, I gotta find someone else." Too bad Dad had retired and left for the greener and warmer pastures of Florida, because I could really use a yes right now.

I mentally ran through my close friends. Cal's schedule was too unpredictable, but Hannah was an option. We weren't close, but she was family. "Antonio Ricci, must be serious if you're calling me."

"It is." I explained what I needed and crossed my fingers. "Can you help me out?"

"I want to say yes, but I have a big delivery arriving tomorrow and my house will be a kid-free zone for the next week or so. Sorry. Maybe I can take half a shift and stay with her at your place?"

It wasn't ideal, but if it was my only option I would make it work. "All right Hannah, thanks. Let me make a couple more calls and I'll let you know."

"Cool." She ended the call abruptly and I laughed at finding someone with worse phone manners than mine.

There was one more option and I sucked in a deep breath, let it out slowly and dialed. "Ollie, I need a huge favor." I went through the whole tale once again and begged for his help. "It's just for a day. I leave tomorrow night and I'll be back the day after."

"I can do it. I might not have been present during the important years, but I remember how to take care of tykes when they're Rosie's age. Keep 'em safe, fed, clean and happy."

My shoulders sank in relief. "Thanks Ollie. I owe you one."

"Nah, you don't. That's what friends are for and it's a good lesson I'm glad to see you're finally learning. Maybe if I had asked for help back in the day, I wouldn't have lost so many years with Augusta." The sadness in the old man's voice was a punch to the gut.

"I had a good teacher drill that lesson into me until it became second nature."

He laughed. "Nice of you to say."

"It's not nice, it's the truth. I'll even share this story at the next meeting."

"Good. Good. I'll see you tomorrow for dinner then."

"Perfect. Thank you, Ollie."

"None necessary," he said again, his voice a low grumble that said the man still didn't know how to accept kind words. "I'll keep your girl safe."

"I know you will." As soon as I got off the phone with Ollie, I texted his daughter. "Cooking lesson number two tonight?"

Her response came back almost immediately. "More lessons? I'm a salad dressing expert now, and as such, I've learned all I can from your culinary brain. But thanks for the offer."

I shook my head before I came up with the perfect response. "Then you can show me everything you've learned by cooking me dinner. Tonight at eight. That should give you plenty of time to plan something to wow the pants off me."

"An ice cold beer could do that."

Damn I loved this woman's wit and the way she didn't try to spare my ego. Ever. "I'll bring the beer. Eight o'clock, Augusta."

She responded with three eyeroll emojis.

"Don't hesitate to call if you need any tips or tricks. I'm full of them."

More emojis, this time crying laughing ones. "You're full of something. Eight o'clock."

Her easy acceptance surprised me a bit, and I

wondered if that meant she was starting to see things my way. Pleasure didn't have to be meaningless, and tonight was the perfect night to show her that.

Gus

✿

"Pizza is fine. Pizza is *more* than fine considering he just invited himself to dinner." I stood at the kitchen counter, covered in flour while I chatted with Megan.

"You could have said no," she offered with a hint of humor in her voice. "But you agreed, so some part of you must want to entertain him for a night. Maybe more."

I scoffed. "I just figured that agreeing would end whatever this is sooner rather than later."

"I don't know, Gus. It sounds like it might be the beginning to me." Megan's sing-song tone made me smile despite myself as I wrapped the pizza dough to let it rise while I showered and got changed.

"Beginning of what? Antonio's newfound interest in me is out of boredom, and it will pass soon enough." I wasn't sure of much when it came to Antonio Ricci, but I was certain that his interest in me wouldn't last.

"I wouldn't be so sure," Megan offered on a sigh. "I've known Antonio most of my life so don't let the bad boy image fool you. He's sweet and kind, and more than capable of commitment."

"Oh please, Megan. Even if I believed that, I've seen photos of his ex-wife. If, and that's a big *if*, Antonio settles down again, it'll be with someone beautiful and glamorous, not someone spends most of her days in scrubs."

"Shut up, you're gorgeous and you know it. More importantly, Antonio seems to know it, so why don't you just enjoy having the attention of a handsome man, and maybe get yourself laid in the process."

"That's just what I plan to do, eat some good pizza, drink a beer or two, all while I have some Grade A eye candy to ogle while I do it."

"Good girl," Megan replied. "Tell me the details tomorrow over coffee?"

"Sure."

Almost two hours later, I was freshly showered, dressed in snug but relaxed fit jeans with a hole in one thigh, a pink t-shirt and flip flops. It was feminine but casual, because I didn't want to look like I was trying to look good and I didn't want Antonio to think that.

The dough had risen and the pizza ingredients were just about ready to go, salami, onions, mushrooms and bell peppers with three types of cheese. A six pack of beer sat chilling in the fridge and the butterflies in my stomach were mostly under control.

The dough was pre-cooking in the oven when the doorbell rang and I let out a long exhale. Antonio's face met me with a smile when the door opened.

"Casual, but sexy," he growled. "I approve."

I rolled my eyes and took a step back. "Great, now I can die a happy woman."

"Happy," he purred and stepped inside with a predatory grin. "But not satisfied. Not yet."

I couldn't help but laugh. "You're always on, aren't you?"

"Not always, no. There's just something about you that brings out the flirt in me, Augusta."

"The kitchen is straight back, just follow the smell."

"What's for dinner?"

"Ah, the important stuff. Right?"

"Damn straight. Food is what fuels us, what stimulates us. It's what brings us together."

"Wow, a poet too? Now I am impressed." I didn't expect him to speak so eloquently about food. I guess I figured he just cooked because he was good at it, but it seemed like cooking and creating dishes was just part of who Antonio is.

"I am more than just a pretty face, Augusta. Sooner or later you'll figure that out." His long legs carried him straight to the stove to inspect the ingredients that sat warming on the stove. "Pizza? I approve."

"Be still my beating heart." I didn't make pizza to please him, I made it just to make sure he wasn't impressed. "Pizza was what I had time for, but I did make the dough. My teacher said to let it rise for three hours but I'm a working woman and ninety minutes got the job done."

"I guess we'll see, won't we?" The teasing glint in his eyes made my belly clinch and pulse, a sensation I ignored.

"Even bad pizza is good pizza, right?" I crossed to the fridge, eager for a break from the eye candy I was so hungry for just a few moments ago. "Beer?"

"Sure. I brought amber ale, what do you have?"

I shrugged. "German black beer. Which do you want?"

"I'll try yours first."

I turned to the fridge and let the chill from within do its thing for my overheated skin. The weight of Antonio's gaze, even when I was looking back, was heavy like a lover's grope. I took my time reaching for two bottles of beer, letting out a silent sigh before turning to face him again.

"Here we go, two beers while the pizza bakes."

"Thanks. How was your day, Augusta?"

I blinked, confused by the switch from flirt to gent. "Um, good?"

He laughed and shook his head. "I'm not a monster, you know."

"I know. It's just, you don't seem like the *how's your day* sort of guy," I told him honestly. "My day was good. Busy as it always is, but I didn't get puked or peed on, and one of the long-term patients was discharged, so it was not bad overall. How was yours?"

Antonio leaned forward with a slow smile. "Do you want me to tell you, or do you want to be surprised along with the rest of my...fans?"

"Walked right into that one, didn't I?"

"You did." Damn that smile was as irresistible as they came, especially when its full force was directed right at me. "Just admit that you like me."

"What's not to like, Antonio? I like looking at you, and listening to you talk. I like watching you cook. I even like sparring with you."

"I hear a *but* coming."

"But," I started and raised both eyebrows. "You're a heartbreaker."

"I'm not," he insisted. Antonio shook his head, a bittersweet smile on his gorgeous face. "In fact, the last time I let my heart get involved, it was my heart that got broken."

"Really?"

"Really," he shot back with another smile. "I loved Trishelle, at least I thought I did. Turns out she loved drugs more than she ever loved me or Rosie."

I listened, rapt, as he told me all about his marriage to Trishelle. "But she seems to put together."

"That's the Hollywood lie. A coat of face paint and some designer clothes can make anyone seem like they have their shit together, especially with a high dollar production crew on the job." His tone turned bitter. "I was foolish enough to think she'd settled down after we were married, but it got worse. And then it got better, when she was pregnant with Rosie."

"That's good," I offered, but I already knew their love story ended in divorce which meant clearly something had gone badly wrong.

"It was. Until it wasn't. At first she loved being a mom, Rosie was her little doll to dress up and photograph all day long. Until the asthma problems began. Then she couldn't or wouldn't, cope." His brown eyes slammed shut, like he was stuck in the past, reliving those memories. "I found her overdosed on the sofa while Rosie was blue in the face from lack of oxygen. My heart broke thinking my little girl would die, and then to think the woman I loved, my wife, was responsible? It killed me."

I couldn't help it, I reached out to Antonio. Perhaps it was the nurse in me who couldn't stand to see another person in so much pain, or maybe it was the sight of this big strong man, near tears over his precious little daughter.

"Rosie is all good now and she's where she belongs, with her daddy."

Antonio nodded and took a moment to get himself back under control. He was probably already regretting he'd shared so much. "You're right, she is where she belongs. And I love to hear you say 'daddy'."

Thankfully the oven timer sounded in all of its loud, obnoxious glory. "Saved by the buzzer."

"The buzzer is temporary. Daddy is forever."

I froze at his words, at just how ridiculous he was, but I knew it was for my benefit. An overt attempt on his part to lighten the mood. And I understood. More than that, I laughed. Hard and loud and long, I laughed until I doubled over with it while the buzzer continued to sound just a few feet away. "You, are...," I gasped but the laughter was uncontrollable and I couldn't speak.

Antonio's chair scraped against the floor and a moment later, he brushed past me. "I'm hilarious? Handsome? Sexy as hell? Thank you."

"You're delusional, my friend."

He turned to me in surprise. "We're friends? Good to know." Antonio turned away again, and I realized what he was doing, and that stopped my laughter.

"Hey, that's my dinner you're screwing up over there!"

"Screwing up? You have a famous chef in your kitchen, and you think I'll be the one to screw things up?"

"Damn right."

"Well you were too busy laughing it up, and now I'm over here. What are you going to do, pick me up and move me out of your way?" There was a hint of challenge and a hint of teasing in the way he looked at me, the way he folded his arms as if I couldn't move him.

"I could pick you up and move you. If I wanted to. But I wouldn't want to bruise your fragile male ego."

"I can handle it. So can my ego."

"That's what you say now, but when your feet are off the ground you'll be grumbling a different tune."

I knew, instantly, it was a mistake to challenge Antonio's manhood. He closed the distance between us, pizza dough and topping totally forgotten as he got in my face, stood toe-to-toe with me.

"Go ahead, Augusta. Do it."

"I will." I could. If I wanted to.

"I'm waiting." Heat flared in his eyes and I wondered if it was the thought of me picking him up or if he felt the heat and electricity that swirled between us. "Tick tock, sweetheart."

"Sweetheart?" I sucked in a breath and before I could let it out, Antonio's thick lips were pressed against mine, his big hands, warm through my t-shirt, settled on my shoulders for a brief moment before sliding down my arms to my waist. They came to a stop at my hips and he pulled me close, slid his tongue back and forth across the seam of my lips, gently begging me to let him in.

I thought about it while I savored the feel of his capable mouth and talented hands gripping me like I was the irresistible one. I could lean into this kiss. I could keep my eyes closed and just go with the flow, take what he was offering, what I wanted, without looking back.

Yeah, that sounded nice.

Hell, it sounded right.

Why couldn't I end my dry spell with Antonio? He wasn't looking for serious, and it didn't have to be. It could just be fun, or like Antonio said, pleasure for the sake of pleasure. I hadn't had any pleasure, at least none brought by a living, breathing male, in a long time. And even then, he wasn't nearly as masculine or as potent as the man who'd slipped between my lips on a breathless sigh.

His big hands slid from my hips to my ass, and he pulled me right up against the long hard ridge of his erection. Antonio kissed me deeper, his touches grew hungrier and harder.

I pulled back and smiled, looked up at him with wide eyes. "Antonio," I panted.

"Right here, Augusta. Right here and ready for another taste."

Oh yeah, he was ready all right. His brown eyes were dark with desire, his nostrils flared and his hands gripped my hips tighter and tighter, the feel of his cock pressed against my stomach teased me. Tempted me.

Holy hell did it tempt me!

He stood there, patient while I decided whether to pump the brakes or slam on the gas. His hands moved up, and his thumbs found an exposed strip of flesh between my shirt and waistband, and teased me. "Fuck," I growled and jumped in his arms, not self-conscious about whether or not he could hold me, just determined to get another taste for myself.

While he steadied himself and gripped my waist, I held his face and devoured his mouth, tasting every corner until I was satisfied I had it memorized. My tongue slid across his straight teeth, the ridges on the roof of his mouth, the bumps and grooves on his tongue, every inch left me hot.

Bothered.

Turned on.

Tantalized.

"Augusta," he growled when he ripped his mouth from mine and smiled. "You're driving me crazy."

"Yeah?" Even in my haze of lust it was hard to believe, but I felt just how hard he was between my thighs.

"Hell yeah."

"Good, because this is happening."

Those words were just what Antonio needed to hear. His feet began to move, to carry us towards the living room where he laid me on the sofa and stared down at me. "You sure?"

I nodded. There was a brief hitch of hesitation, but I shoved it down deep. This wasn't about a crush or a future, it was about the here and now. It was about pleasure. "Absolutely sure."

"Good." His hands went to my button and then my zipper, and soon he yanked my jeans down my hips. "I knew you were a frilly lingerie type of girl."

"Did you?"

"I imagined you were, but sheer pink panties? I didn't imagine these." His fingertips slid under and just traced the seam of my thigh until I shook and panted with desire. "I can see your plump pussy lips, and a little strip of hair, it's making me hard."

"You're already hard."

"Harder," he growled and stood so his erection was eye level.

"I see." My hand went to the bulge in his jeans and I rubbed it, gently at first, but faster and harder when I felt more confident. Bolder. "I can feel it too."

"Augusta," he growled and I wrapped my hand tighter around his denim covered erection.

"Antonio." His jaws were clenched tight and I liked it. A lot. I reveled in knowing that I was the one bringing him to the brink of madness. He stared at me for so long that I started to feel bold and sexy. I slid one hand down to my panties, inside them, and found myself wet and swollen. One slip of my finger and my hips bucked off the sofa.

"Augusta," he dropped to his knees, replacing my hand with his. "Such a wet little pussy. So fucking plump too." I was about to object to his use of the word plump, but his next words stopped me dead. "Those fat lips will feel so good brushing against my cock when I pump into you."

"Yes, please." The words came out husky and breathless, surely they couldn't belong to me. I didn't get breathless over men.

"Please. I like that." He yanked off my panties and spread my legs so he could gaze down at my most intimate spot. "So pink. So pretty," he whispered before he slid one finger deep into me, smiling when my back arched from the sensation. He added another finger and smiled. "What a tight little pussy."

He talked so much, and damn him, I couldn't deny the dirty talk turned me on as much as his fingers. "It's been...a while."

"How long?"

"A while," I shot back, reluctant to discuss that now. Or ever.

"So you really need to cum?"

"I would like very much to cum, Antonio."

He teased me with shallow pumps, his thumb grazed over my clit so swiftly I might have imagined the touch. "You're close."

"I'm not," I insisted because I wasn't. It took me ages to get off, probably why most men stopped trying after a while.

"You are," he shot back and leaned forward until his breath fanned the strip of hair I kept neat and tidy even though no one but me had seen it in half a year. Then his mouth was on me, his tongue flicked over my clit while his fingers thrust in and out at a frenetic pace that suffused my body with heat.

"Antonio," I moaned as my fingers found themselves tangled in his thick dark hair, my hips rolled against the touch of his mouth.

He responded with a growl that sent vibrations all the way up my spine, and a moment later his lips and tongue sucked my clit. The dueling sensations of soft lips and tongue combined with thrusting fingers was more than enough to send me right over the edge. In a minute, maybe two. "Yeah, I knew you were close."

"You didn't *know* anything. You guessed."

"I knew," he insisted and swirled his tongue around my clit one final time, a move that made my hips buck again. He smiled and sat back with a smug look on his face before he brought his fingers to his mouth and licked them clean. "You were so slick, and your clit so swollen, I knew you were close."

"It usually takes me longer."

"That's because I'm not usually here."

"Arrogant."

"Confident."

"Right." I rolled my eyes and sat up, or tried to, but Antonio put a hand to my chest and pushed me back down. "What are you doing?"

He flashed another of those animalistic smiles and took of my t-shirt and bra before he stood. "I'm about to give you what we both want, Augusta."

I swallowed at the sight of Antonio, undressing in my living room. He was built as hell, long lean muscles and colorful tattoos everywhere. "You're beautiful." The words slipped out before I could stop them.

"Right back atcha, babe." He winked before he covered my body with his. "I'll go slow just in case you can't handle it."

I rolled my eyes. "Oh!" But dammit, he was right. Antonio was big. And thick. And I really liked it. A lot. "I can handle it if you can."

"You're...tight," he grunted as his cock sank deeper to the point of discomfort. "All right?"

"More than," I assured him and tightened my thighs around his waist, digging my heels into his tight ass. "Yeah, I'm all right."

"Excellent." He grunted again when I tightened and pulsed around him to assure him I could handle what he wanted to give me. Pleasure, and his big fat cock.

Watching Antonio was even more erotic than watching him cook. His brows were bunched in focus, jaws clenched with restraint even as he stroked slow and deep into me. He filled me up deliciously, so thick I could hardly breathe, and I wanted it. All of it. "More, Antonio. Give me more." His strokes were still slow and deep, so I did what any woman would. "Please." I begged.

"Augusta," he growled in my ear. "You know what that does to me."

"I do."

He smiled and pushed at the back of my thighs, pumping harder and deeper from this new angle and I thought I might die from the sensations ricocheting around my body. He was a work of art, bunching and flexing as he pounded into me.

"Yes!" I reached out and gripped his thigh as I fought to keep my eyes open because I didn't want to miss one moment of this .

He smiled and let my legs fall so he could lean over, lick my breasts as he thrust into me over and over. Fast and hard and deep, exactly what I needed. "Fuck. Augusta."

Unbelievably, another orgasm approached, fast and intense. My fingertips dug deep into him and I arched into him, tightened my legs around him. "Antonio!" Pleasure crashed over me like a wave, weighing me down while each wave came one right after the other.

All the while, Antonio's hips never stopped. He thrusted and pounded, harder, until a telltale growl erupted from deep within him. "Augusta." He collapsed on top of me, his hips still moved in slow shallow strokes.

"Wow. Just...wow."

He laughed against me, the sound bouncing from his chest to mine and back again until my nipples hardened and I convulsed around him. "I'll take wow and give one right back to you. That was better than my dreams. Almost."

"Almost?"

He nodded. "In my dreams I watched while you sucked me off."

I sucked in a breath at his words, the image immediately at the forefront of my mind. Me down on my knees while he sat here on the sofa, dark eyes flaring with heat and desire. Dark and hungry. *Pleasure for pleasure's sake,* I reminded myself and smiled.

"Maybe after pizza, you'll get your wish."

"Is that the oven I hear?"

Totally naked with him still buried in me, I laughed.

Antonio groaned as I squeezed around him involuntarily. "Augusta."

"I was promised pizza. Get to work, chef." I gave his ass a smack and Antonio laughed.

"Now you want me to screw up your pizza?"

I nodded. "You managed to get this part right, I'm sure you can trust you with a bit of dough."

He smiled at the challenge and leaned forward to lick a trail of heat across my jaw. "I can handle more than the pizza," he growled and I felt him harden inside of me.

Thirty, maybe forty minutes later, we got around to the pizza.

And later, we got around to fulfilling another fantasy for us both.

Antonio

"Antonio! You're looking as hot as ever, and this look is even turning me on." Magda fanned her face with her hand and rolled her eyes. "You sure you don't want to stay a few days? I could get you some high paid photo work. With those cheekbones and tattoos, I could probably even get you on somebody's runway."

It took me about a year to figure out that Magda wasn't flirting, the woman was just brutally honest in both directions. "If you can squeeze something in before I leave for Oregon, fine. Otherwise I have to get back to Rosie."

"That right there," she pointed at my chest. "That whole good dad thing combined with this packaging, I could make us both some good money, Antonio."

"Then what are you waiting for?" I would never

turn down the opportunity to make money and increase my channel's exposure, as long as I didn't have to stay away from my daughter for too long.

"I'm on it," she promised and pulled out her phone just as a production assistant grabbed me and pulled me onto the cooking show set. Magda waved as she smiled into the phone.

"This is Antonio Ricci," the assistant introduced me to Wallace Young and Akana Murphy, two popular chefs who found alternative paths to culinary success.

"Nice to meet you both. Akana, I had your kimchi breakfast burrito on my way to the set."

She smiled proudly. "And?"

"It was incredible. The pork sausage was a fantastic addition."

"I thought so too." She smiled and was about to say something when the director interrupted us.

"Make sure you keep up a steady, but not too loud dialogue during the competition. Observe what the chefs are doing, offer up guesses about what they're making and offer your own unique spins on the flavor profiles. Got it?"

We all nodded and offered a polite smile to the abrasive man in the flannel shirt.

"Great. Oh and thanks for being here." The words were an afterthought but it didn't matter. We were all here for one thing. Exposure.

"Dick," Wallace muttered under his breath and

turned to me and Akana. "Don't forget to throw in a few phrases like, *in my restaurant,* or *on my food truck* to make this shoot worth it. *In my book I describe how to do this even for the home cook.* Sounds more organic and not like you're just here to promote yourself."

His advice surprised me. "Thanks, man."

"No problem. Thanks for the shout out on my puffed tofu technique."

"Saw that, did you?"

He laughed. "Got tagged in thousands of Instagram photos thanking us both, that's how I found the video."

I shrugged off his unintended compliment. "Even my kid loves the stuff, just needs ketchup and mustard according to her."

Conversation mostly continued like that for the rest of the day, only focused on the four rounds of competition. The competitors were talented and innovative, and though the director was a dick, the shoot was more fun than I thought it would be.

And a hell of a lot longer.

"My ass is sore," Akana complained as soon we wrapped filming. "I gotta go walk off these calories, see you guys around." With a feminine finger wave, she sauntered off, already on her phone.

"I have to get going too," Wallace offered for no apparent reason. "But I think we should do a cross-over shoot before you head back west. I'm filming in the morning, a steak video. Want to join me?"

"Hell yeah, man. Sounds good. When and where?"

Wallace flashed a satisfied smile and gave me the details. "I'm not a huge stickler for time, but don't be a dick and keep me waiting all day."

"My schedule is tight tomorrow, my flight leaves at four so I'll be on time."

"Perfect. Send my PA your links so we can start doing promo and I'll see you in the A.M."

When I left the studio, Magda took off with a promise to call later and I skipped the row of cabs waiting and decided to walk. I hadn't been to New York for years, and I wanted to enjoy the sights and sounds of the city. More than that, I wanted to see what the new culinary scene looked like, so I stopped at about a dozen different restaurants to hit up some old friends and talk food with likeminded people.

When I left the last restaurant, I had at least sixty ideas typed out on a notepad app, and I was eager to sketch out a new production schedule to incorporate the ideas while they were fresh in my mind.

"Oh my god, Antonio! Is that you?"

I froze at that grating, phoney voice that I knew better than I wanted to, and I turned slowly.

"Trishelle."

She pushed her red painted lips out into a pout. "Is that any way to greet your ex-wife?"

"She's lucky I'm greeting her at all. What are you

doing here?" I was instantly on edge, wondering if this was somehow a setup.

"Me? Oh, I'm just here to get some shopping in for the week. What are you doing here?"

"Working," I grunted and looked around the street for cameras or boom mics, or some of her reality show minions. "Well, take care of yourself Trishelle."

She took a step closer and then another and put her hands on my chest. "That's it? Not even a nice to see you again, or you're looking well babe?" She pouted again and looked up at me. "How about we get a late meal and catch up."

I took a step back, out of her reach and shook my head. "No thanks. I'm busy."

"How's Rosie?"

"She's good. Happy." And I wanted to keep it that way. "How's your sobriety?" It didn't take an expert to see she was on something, probably pills and booze, at the moment.

Those words had the desired effect. "Fuck you, Antonio. You think you're so much better than me, but you're not."

"I don't think anything about you anymore, Trishelle."

She smiled and reached out to me again, her smile darkened when I pushed her hands away. "You wish that was the case, don't you?" She smiled over her shoulder and that's when I knew this was most definitely a setup.

"No, because it is the truth. How can I want a woman back who almost killed my daughter?"

"Our daughter." She growled and stepped in close. "Don't forget that."

I laughed loudly, just in case she thought of using this footage for some nefarious reason. "Yeah, when was the last time you've seen *our* daughter? Not since you lost custody, so go sell your lies to someone who doesn't know you. And if you think I'm signing a release, you'd better think again."

She sucked in an outraged breath and turned on her four-inch stilettos before she stormed off, probably perfectly planned from the outset.

I shook my head and shoved my hands in my pockets before I took off in the opposite direction, happy to get out of this interaction with my ex without getting the cops involved. It was another reminder that I made the right decision when I divorced Trishelle, took Rosie and left Los Angeles. There was too much drama in that world, too many opportunities to make the wrong choices, the kind that could cost me my kid. My career.

As soon as I made it back to my hotel room, I called Rosie. "Hey Princess, how are you?"

"Hi Daddy! I'm good, and I'm behaving for Mr.

Ollie. Me and Nurse Gus are making cookies. With chocolate and gummies and sours."

I winced at her list and shook my head. "Sounds delicious."

Rosie giggled. "Nurse Gus said it sounds gross, but princesses are the boss so I got to choose."

"Did she?"

"Uh-huh. And we made hero sandwiches for dinner. I got to pick what I wanted too, like a big girl."

I smiled as Rosie talked until she was breathless, telling me about her entire day in fifteen minute increments. "Sounds like you're having fun without me."

"I miss you Daddy, but you'll be back tomorrow, right?"

"You know I can't stay away from you for too long, Princess."

"I know," she shouted and then gasped. "My cookies are done, Daddy. Gotta go!" The phone fell to the ground and I heard Ollie groan.

"That girl of yours has more energy than ten children. God love her, but if I could bottle that energy and sell it, I'd be a rich man. Rich enough to split the proceeds with you." He let out a rusty laugh that made me smile.

"Thanks again, Ollie."

"Don't thank me, thank Augusta. She showed up after her shift and she's been helping me all day. Not sure if it's because she doesn't trust me with her, or if she wants to spend time with me. Either way, I'll take it."

"Did she say that she doesn't trust you with Rosie?"

"No," he grunted. "But she must have better things to do than help her old man babysit."

"Emphasis on old, Ollie. Maybe she was worried you'd overdo it with Rosie, and it sounds like she was right to worry. You sound exhausted."

"I'm always exhausted," he insisted. "I'm old."

"Exactly."

"Yeah, yeah. See you tomorrow."

Hearing my daughter's voice and talking to Ollie, were just more signs that I did the right thing by moving back to Jackson's Ridge. Where else could my little girl have a surrogate grandfather happy to pitch in at the last minute to help out? She was thriving in my hometown, and so was I. I needed the reassurance after my run in with my ex-wife, and I got that with just one phone call to Jackson's Ridge.

It was fun to do these small trips to get a taste of the life I gave up, to spend a little time in someone else's kitchen and make a little cash in the process. It was a nice little vacation, but I couldn't wait to get back to Rosie.

To Jackson's Ridge.

To Augusta.

Gus

❧❧❧

"Antonio. What are you doing here?" It was a nice surprise to open the door and find the sexy chef on my doorstep wearing a sultry smile that went perfectly with his jeans and white t-shirt, a look that only made his tattoos look more vibrant and stunning.

He leaned forward with heat in his eyes, bracing muscled arms on my doorframe. "I came to see you. To say hi. Hi." His voice was low and deep, and hit me right between the thighs, just as he intended no doubt.

"Hi." His bold moves always made me feel like a shy girl, but the heat in his gaze reminded me that I was all woman. "Want to come in?"

Antonio nodded as he stepped inside, his chest brushed against mine which forced me to move back. His lips pulled into a smile that grew closer and closer before his mouth crashed down over mine. His kiss was hot and hungry, his hands held my face like I was someone he cherished, like I meant something to him.

I groaned at the way his tongue tangled with mine and slid my hands up and across his strong back, let my fingers explore the ridges of muscle and bone until my finger tips curled into his thick, dark hair. "Hi." That one word came out breathless. And happy. "How was New York?"

"Good."

"Good?" I folded my arms. "That's all I get?" I didn't expect him to open his heart up to me, but a little conversation wasn't out of the question. Was it?

"Nope. I'll tell you everything. Over dinner." He took a step backwards and returned to the porch to pick up two canvas sacks. "I'm cooking."

"How can I turn down a meal cooked by a handsome chef?"

His lips twitched before he unleashed a crooked smile that had the butterflies in my stomach doing somersaults. "A handsome professional chef, you mean?"

"Yeah, all that," I told him with a wave of my hands. "The kitchen is that way."

"Oh, I remember exactly where the kitchen is. And the living room." His gaze fell on the sofa as he passed the living room, and he no doubt had the same thoughts I had whenever I looked the sofa since our night together. "Can't forget that sofa. Ever."

Yeah, I couldn't either. Unfortunately. This thing wouldn't last forever, but that sofa was just two years old and I didn't want to think of Antonio every time I looked at it. "Kitchen, straight ahead."

He laughed again. "How do you feel about dumplings?"

"I love them. What kind?"

"Shrimp and pork. I'll teach you how to make the wrappers, it's easy."

"Easy," I rolled my eyes. "You chefs always say that, and so rarely is anything involving dough easy. So rarely."

"Trust me?"

I nodded because I did trust Antonio, at least when it came to food. The way my heart raced as he smiled at me, and my thighs tightened when he licked his lips, told me that I couldn't trust him or me when it came to my heart. "Fine. Beer?"

"Isn't that how we ended up naked last time?"

"No," I laughed. "Pretty sure it was because I threatened to pick you up, and that, for some reason, got you all hot and bothered."

"It wasn't the threat, it was the woman." The heat in his gaze sent a shiver down my spine and I went to the fridge, stuck my head inside for a long moment before I pulled back with two beers.

"So, tell me about New York."

"Bossy. I like it." Antonio smiled and unloaded the ingredients on my counter before he got to work and I settled on one of the stools on the opposite side of the island. I settled in to enjoy the sight of him at work. "New York was short and sweet. I filmed a cooking segment with Wallace Young, which was pretty amazing."

"The guy who mixes cuisine types to create crazy dishes?"

"You know him? Yeah, he's a crazy son of a bitch, but also a genius." The fondness and awe in his voice told me a lot about Antonio as a chef.

"You really are one of those dig your hands in the dirt and taste leaves kind of chef, aren't you?" I pegged him all wrong, at least on that account. "The real deal."

"Disappointed?"

"No. Yes. Maybe." The fact that he was genuine would make it harder to keep my distance, but it was good to know he wasn't just some leather-clad, tattooed poser.

"Good."

I took a long pull from my beer bottle and sighed. "Yeah? Why?"

"Because it means you're seeing me in a different light. And because it's giving me some insight into who you are, Augusta."

"Me? I'm an open book."

"Not all the time. I know you're a nurse who works with children, you care a lot and you're a smart ass. Other than Ollie being your dad, I know almost nothing about you. Do you have a mother?"

I laughed. "Don't we all?"

He dipped his head and gave me a look.

"Okay, yes I have a mother. She walked out when I was twelve years old and I haven't seen her since."

His hands stopped moving. "I'm sorry to hear that. Is that why you understand Rosie?"

I shrugged. "Maybe. But I am kind of an expert in children, specifically sick children whose parents find it difficult to let them grow up too soon."

"You're right about that, I want to keep her a little girl for as long as possible."

"I know, but dealing with illness as a kid, no matter who's illness, makes you grow up a little faster." Many times it was unavoidable, but even when it was, there was no way to stop a child from maturing too fast with mature situations to deal with everyday.

"Sounds like you speak from personal experience."

I sighed and nodded. My childhood wasn't something I talked about to most people, but Antonio had been honest with me about the breakdown of his marriage, his fears about Rosie. I could do this.

"My father fell into a bottle when my mom walked out on us, or maybe she walked out *because* of his drinking, I'm not sure. All I know is that it worsened after she left, and it was up to me to take care of all the things he couldn't or wouldn't. I grew up fast and it made me independent, paying bills, keeping the house presentable, signing report cards, and pretty much anything I could to avoid being put in foster care."

"That sounds rough." He was sympathetic but not surprised, and *that* surprised me.

"It was an experience, for sure. It taught me how to take care of myself, to rely on myself. But it also led to years of estrangement between me and Dad. He resented me for what I did, and I resented him for putting me in that position." I hated to think about that time, of losing touch with my only family and being truly alone for the first time in my life. "But things are better now. With him here in town, he seems happy and I'm happy to have him in my life again."

"Are you?"

"Yep. I asked him to move here because I wanted a chance to fix things between us. For both of us."

"Did you ask because he's sober now?"

I blinked. "Who said he was sober?"

"I worked in the restaurant industry, Augusta, you think I don't know an addict when I see one? I never would have let Ollie take care of her if he was still drinking."

"Right, of course not. You knew."

He nodded. "I did."

"But, how?"

Antonio broke the rhythmic moves of stuffing and folding dumplings and looked at me. "Ollie leads a single parent support group at the community center and he talks openly about his mistakes."

"Oh."

"Yeah. Being a single parent is hard, and it's even harder when you have obstacles like a sick kid or an addict in the family. It's damn hard." He shook his head, and shoulders fell with what seemed like regret. "It took me too long to make the decision to leave the long hours in the kitchen behind for Rosie's sake. If I was a better man, a better father it would have been a no-brainer."

"Maybe." I understood where he was coming from. In the hospital there are rarely good choices, only the less bad option. "But how would you have taken care of Rosie and her healthcare bills without a job? Kids require money and resources, and sick kids need even more."

He flashed another of those heart stopping smiles and nodded. "True, but I should have been working on a way to earn a living outside the kitchen much sooner than I did. As soon as I found her half-dead with Trishelle."

"Well, you made the choice in the end, and Rosie is better for it. Isn't that what matters?"

"I suppose." He didn't want the compliment, which only meant he deserved it more. The man who was usually so arrogant, couldn't take a compliment on his skills and choices as a parent. Was there anything hotter than a man who wanted nothing more than to be a good dad?

"Trust me?"

He smiled. "Sure thing. In fact, I'm trusting you to make the dipping sauce."

"Me?"

He nodded. "It's only fair, right?"

"I don't know about fair, but I'm always up for learning a new dipping sauce. Tell me what to do, chef."

His gaze darkened and he licked his lips. "I love it when you talk dirty to me, Augusta." He barked out a laugh when I rolled my eyes at him. "Okay, first step, take off your shirt."

I knew he was joking, but I did it anyway. "Okay. Next step?"

"Augusta," he growled.

"Did you forget the next step, Chef?"

His gaze darkened and he put his hands on his hips, eyes focused on my cleavage. "Pants."

Feeling bold, I kept my eyes on him as I slid them over my hips and down my legs. "Next."

Antonio let out a low growl and turned away from me, gripping the edge of the sink like he was searching for restraint. That was the exact opposite of what I wanted from him in the moment. He turned on the hot water and washed his hands for almost a full minute before he turned back to me. "Holy shit, Augusta."

I stood there with my hands on my hips, wearing nothing but a smile. "What should I do next, Chef?"

He licked his lips and closed the distance between us quickly. "Me." He devoured my mouth and lifted me in the air, gripped my ass until I wrapped my legs around him.

"Gladly," I growled and took control of the kiss. Feeling bold and sexy, I kissed him long and hard, ground my hips against him until his control snapped.

Antonio carried me to the bedroom and tossed me on the bed, eyes fixed on the jiggle of my breasts. It was tantalizing, being the sole focus of that heated gaze. I wanted to see him lose control, and I did everything in my power to make it happen.

He was so beautiful, face twisted in erotic agony as I took him in my mouth. I watched him carefully as I pleased him, every swipe of my tongue, every suck, giving me the key to driving him crazy.

By the time I straddled his hips and rode his cock, Antonio finally gave me what I wanted. His control snapped and his big hands gripped me hard, almost too hard, as he pounded up into me. His mouth scrambled to taste my skin, his hands kneaded and squeezed my breasts as they bounced with every stroke.

It was so good, so all-encompassing that I could hardly stand it. I felt my walls crumbling with the pleasure, the words he spoke as pleasure swamped him. "So good, babe. So fucking good," he growled and held me close to him, his strokes hit me so deep I saw stars.

His teeth sank into the crook of my neck and I came harder than I ever had before.

Antonio

I was hooked. I couldn't get Augusta off my mind, especially after everything that happened two nights ago. She was a fucking breath of fresh air, giving me things I didn't even know I wanted or needed. She was sweet and hot, an irresistible combination that I couldn't get enough of. Not yet anyway.

I would get enough of her, eventually, but for now, all I wanted was Augusta. Every time I had her, I wanted her again.

Yeah, I was done for.

"Earth to Antonio." Teddy waved her hand in front of my face, a knowing smile on her face. "Oh there you are. Thought we lost you to dreamland for a minute."

"What are you doing here, Teddy?" Not that I didn't love spending time with my only sister, but I didn't expect her today, and her presence put a kink in my plans.

"Good to see you too, bro. I'm here to see my favorite little princess. Is that all right?"

"Yeah, of course. In fact, it's perfect." I needed to make a quick run, and it would be easier if Rosie wasn't there.

"Yeah?" Teddy sat back and folded her arms, a wide toothy smile splitting her face. "What is it that you have to do, dear brother?"

"Something personal. Nothing for you to concern yourself about. Can you keep an eye on Rosie for a little bit?"

"Yep. Cal's shift just started and Hannah is busy, so my afternoon is pretty wide open. Later I have plans, though, so don't think you can disappear all day."

"I wouldn't dream of it." My errand shouldn't take much time at all, but I could linger knowing that Rosie was being looked after. "I'll be back in an hour."

Teddy's dark brows arched, a question burned in her eyes. "Going to see Gus?"

Was I that transparent? "Maybe."

"You are! Holy crap, you totally are going to see Gus!" Big brown eyes, nearly identical to my own, stared at me in wide-eyed shock and surprise. And glee. "So you guys really are seeing each other?"

"I don't know about all that. We've been spending time together. Having fun." Things weren't serious.

Sure, I was a little taken with the pretty pediatric nurse, but we were dating and we weren't serious. "Don't make it more than it is, Teddy."

She held her hands up in a defensive gesture. "I'm not making it anything, merely asking a question."

"Right." I didn't believe my sister for one second, but I didn't have time to argue. "Gotta go." I kissed Teddy's cheek and gave Rosie a tight hug and kiss before I hurried out the door.

"Bye, Daddy!"

"Have fun with your aunt!"

"You have fun too," Teddy called after me and I didn't need to look back to see the smile I heard in her voice.

After a quick stop to Petals of Glee, I made my way to the medical center where I was immediately greeted by Melanie's knowing smile. "Antonio, you handsome devil. Where's Rosie?"

I rubbed a hand over my head and flashed a sheepish grin. "She's hanging out with her aunt for a few hours."

"Oh." That one word held a wealth of meaning that I refused to touch. "So you're here for...medical advice?"

"Nope. I'm looking for Augusta, is she around?"

With another knowing smile, Melanie turned to face her computer screen and tapped a few keys before she turned back to me. "She's up on the pediatric floor, checking on patients. Go on up, you'll find her."

"Thanks, Melanie."

"Sure thing, handsome." She waved me off and I had no doubt she would be on the phone, lighting up the gossip line before I set eyes on Augusta.

A pair of hot pink scrubs came into view as I rounded the corner from the elevator, and I don't know how I knew, but I knew it was Augusta. Maybe it was the way the pink scrubs hugged her hips and butt, or the way she crouched down to talk to the crying youngster, but I just knew it was her. I waited patiently for her to finish up with her patient.

This town must be filled with idiots if none of the men in town had seen the gift that was Augusta. She wasn't just kind and caring, and damn good at her job. She was beautiful. Sweet. Hot in the sack.

"Antonio, what are you doing here? Is Rosie all right?" She looked behind me in search of my daughter, and yeah, for just a moment, I thought maybe I more than liked this woman.

"Rosie is fine, hanging out with Teddy."

"Oh." She blinked several times, her shoulders slowly relaxed as my words sank in. "Then why are you here?"

That genuine confusion in her voice, as if she couldn't believe that I would just show up for her, pulled me into her orbit. "I'm here for you. Obviously."

Her gaze slipped to the bouquet of flowers in my hand and then back to my face, her confusion even stronger. "Okay. Why?"

"To give you these, for starters." I pushed the flowers at her in what was certainly not my smoothest moment. "I, uh, hope you like them." Other than Rosie, I hadn't given a woman flowers since high school, and being unsure made me uneasy.

Augusta's plump lips pulled up into a gentle smile. "They're beautiful, Antonio. Thank you." She looked up, red brows still furrowed. "What's the occasion?"

Hell if I knew. "I wanted to see you and I figured you might like some flowers."

Her smile blossomed fully at those words. "I always like flowers, Antonio."

"Do you have time to talk?"

She let out a husky laugh. "Is talk a euphemism, or do you really want to talk?"

I couldn't tell which answer she wanted and I shrugged. "I'll settle for talking, but I'll never pass up a chance to bury myself deep inside you."

She shivered and let out a shaky breath before she quickly recovered. "Come on. We can talk in my office. Just. Talk."

"Whatever you say, sweetheart." I had no plans to seduce her inside the medical center, there were too many eyes, too many wagging tongues and I didn't want

Augusta to get in trouble. But I wouldn't mind a long drink from her sweet mouth.

She dragged me down the corridor and into an office no bigger than a shoebox, where she shut the door and turned to me with a smile. "What did you want to talk about?"

I couldn't think straight while her hands slid up and down my chest and abs, her thumbs grazing the waist-band of my jeans. "I wanted to invite you...ah hell, I can't concentrate when you do that."

Her hands immediately stopped, but her expression was full of mischief, not regret. "Okay. Talk." She took five big steps back, leaving too much distance between us.

"Me and Rosie are going to a Renaissance Fair this weekend and I thought you might like to join us."

I could tell my invitation stunned her because she stood with her mouth open into a perfect 'O', big green eyes stared up at me like she didn't know who I was.

The silence became uncomfortable. "If you don't want to go, just say so..."

Augusta blinked and shook her head. "It's not that, I just wasn't expecting the invitation. But I love history and giant turkey legs, so count me in."

"Perfect." I relaxed with relief, and with the invitation issued and accepted, I was hungry for a taste of her lips. "Just fucking perfect."

"Yeah?"

I nodded. "Hell yeah," I whispered a hot second before my mouth crashed down over hers, devoured her until she panted and clung to me. Her tongue teased my lips and danced with my tongue while her hands roamed my chest and my back. "Augusta, if you don't take a step back, I will take you right here. Right now."

She shivered again and I was half tempted to do just that. "The door doesn't lock."

I growled and buried my face in her neck. "Too bad."

"Maybe later?"

"Definitely later. Definitely," I kissed her one more time before I headed towards the medical center exit with a wide grin and a bit of energy in my step. Later couldn't come soon enough.

"Antonio!" Cal's voice halted my progression and I turned back with a smile.

"Hey man, what's up?"

Cal sighed and shook his head. "It's already been a long day. Tell me you don't have plans tonight. I need a drink or five, and a night with the guys."

"Hell yes," I growled, unaware of just how badly that's what I needed too.

Cal's expression brightened. "Perfect. Nine o'clock work for you?"

"That'll give me enough time to spend a few hours with Rosie and put her to bed. See you then." A night out with the guys was just what I needed to get over my infatuation with sweet Augusta.

Yeah, it was just what I needed.

At least that's what I thought until I showed up at The Outpost to meet Cal and Casey. "What are you two gossiping about?" I swear there was something about being in a relationship that turned even the most stoic of men into chatty, gossiping old ladies.

Casey flashed a wide smile and patted the chair between him and Cal. "You, actually. Have a seat, there's a pitcher on the way."

I took the seat and stared at my friends. We'd all gone to school together from elementary school until graduation. We had all left to pursue our dreams as well, yet somehow, each of us ended up back in Jackson's Ridge. Sitting around The Outpost as if we had never left.

"What's so interesting about me?"

Cal laughed. "All the time you've been spending with Gus, for starters. Tongues are wagging, my friend."

I shook my head and laughed. "Yeah, your tongue is wagging. Are you lobbying for the biggest gossip in town award?"

"That's a low blow," Casey offered with a laugh.

"I never say no to an award," Cal joked. "But I'm curious. You've been spending a lot of time with Gus lately. Are you seeing each other officially?"

I shrugged off the question with a vague answer. "I wouldn't say that, you know how I feel about labels."

Casey let out a loud bark of laughter. "You didn't just say that, did you?"

"Damn right I did."

Cal sighed. "My poor, ridiculous, fool of a best friend. You can't keep a woman like Gus by stringing her along. She's independent, knows her worth and won't put up with your crap."

"I'm not asking her to." Augusta didn't appear to have a problem with our current, label-less arrangement, and I had no plans to change it. "We'll keep hanging out for as long as it suits both of us."

"So you *do* like her?" Casey asked with a knowing smirk. "Megan said there were serious sparks between you two, but she's a romantic so you can never be sure what she actually saw."

There were definitely sparks. More than sparks. When me and Augusta were together, it was always the pre-cursor to an inferno, hot and bright and seemingly never-ending. "I'll just say that I like spending time with her. She's beautiful and smart. She's cool."

"Cool? What are we, sixteen?" Casey shook his head and helped the waitress with the glasses when she finally got around to bringing our beer to the table.

"Easy to be so smug when you met your wife in the third grade." For as long as I could remember it was always Casey and Megan, Megan and Casey, joined at the hip. "What do you know about dating?"

"I know that we're too old for your games. You like Augusta, if you didn't, you wouldn't have brought flowers to the hospital today."

"You did?" Cal's eyes went wide with shock and I groaned.

"I did." And thanks to Melanie, the whole damn town knew about it.

"So you definitely like her," Cal insisted. "Maybe more than like her if I had to guess."

"Don't guess, Cal. In fact, don't do anything. Me and Augusta are having fun. Trust me, she knows the score."

I hoped she did, because I wasn't even sure if I knew the score anymore.

Gus

❦

"**M**e *and Augusta are having fun. Trust me, she knows the score.*"

I shouldn't have been eavesdropping, I knew that but I couldn't resist the opportunity to hear what Antonio really thought of me. In my silly little mind, I was sure he would tell his friends that I was an unexpected treat, a nice girl, a sexy woman, or even an adventurous lover. Any of those, no matter how vulgar, would have been preferable to *she knows the score.*

What *was* the score, and who was keeping this score?

More importantly, what was the game that we were playing? Because I had no damn idea.

A game.

Just as I suspected, it was all a game to him. I was,

as I always suspected, a way to pass the time. To alleviate the boredom of small town life for a man used to the fast pace of big city living.

I knew it. I absolutely knew it, and I let myself get caught up in his words of pleasure and passion. I was angry. Hell yeah, I was angry. At Antonio, sure, but I was really angry at myself. I knew exactly who Antonio was from the outset, a sexy bad boy who just so happened to be a loving single father. I let myself believe that he was someone else because he was good to his daughter and his sister.

I believed what I wanted to believe.

It was the same thing I did for years when it came to Dad. That first year or two after Mom left and he started drinking, I told myself the drinking was just how he coped with losing the love of his life. That forgetting to pay the light bill was grief, not addiction. I lied to myself over and over until it was clear that the drunk passed out on the sofa was simply who Oliver Thompson was now. It wasn't a fluke or a phase, it was reality.

Once I figured that out, I knew it was up to me to take care of both of us, because he wasn't capable of doing it, and I did it. Every day for years until I graduated from high school, I did it all.

It taught me how to take care of myself because there was no one to step in to do it for me. From the age of thirteen I only had myself to rely on. Just me and no one else.

That's what I get for trying to change things.

"Hey Gus, what'll it be?" The bartender at The Outpost, Cyrus, flashed a friendly bearded smile at me and I shook myself from my thoughts. I wouldn't hold a grudge against Antonio, he was who he was, and he didn't need to apologize for it. No, it was my thinking that was the problem. Me.

"Hey Cy, I'll have two beers and a large pitcher of mango margaritas, please."

Cyrus let out a long, low whistle. "Are we drinking away problems, or is this a celebration?"

I shrugged. "Probably a little bit of both, I suppose."

The look of sympathy that flashed in his big blue eyes put me on edge, but it also made me smile. Cy was a big bear of a man, but he was as kind as he was large.

"In that case, have a shot. On the house."

"Thanks." I accepted the clear liquid and the lime wedge with a grateful smile and knocked it back, letting the silver tequila burn its way down my throat until the warm flush of tipsiness calmed my racing heart. "Thanks a lot, Cy." I paid for the drinks and left him a nice tip before making my way back to the table with our drinks.

"Sheesh woman, did you get lost on the way to the bar?" Hannah flashed a toothy grin and arched a brow as if she knew exactly where I was and what I was up to. Teddy and Megan looked up at my arrival, curiosity swimming in their gazes as well.

I shrugged off the looks. "Long line at the bar, and it takes time to make margaritas." It was a little white lie because I wasn't ready to tell the girls what happened.

Megan rested her chin in her hand and wiggled her eyebrows at me. "You sure you didn't get sidetracked by a certain gorgeous chef?"

"I'm sure," I practically growled at her. "Sorry."

Teddy smacked her hands on the round bar table and sighed. "All right Gus, out with it. What did my brother do now?"

"He didn't do anything. Nothing at all. In fact, it's me who's the problem." I wouldn't be one of those women who turned the man into the villain for being who he was.

"What in the hell does that mean?" Hannah's blond brows dipped into an angry mask.

I sighed and took my time to pour the margaritas while I gathered my thoughts. These women were my friends and I wouldn't lie to them, but first a long sip of mango margarita. "It means that I made the same mistake women have been making since the beginning of time. I ignored his words and only paid attention to his actions. I let them guide me when I shouldn't have.

I knew the score, as he put it, and I did. But I fooled myself anyway."

Teddy sucked in an outraged breath. "My brother said that to you?"

"No," I sighed. "Not *to* me. I overheard him telling Cal and Casey that we were just having fun and I knew the score."

"No!" Hannah gasped.

"Yeah, that's what he said it, and I don't blame him. I did, *do*, know the score."

"That's crap and you know it," Teddy insisted. "What did you know, Gus?"

"That Antonio is a heartbreaker. A bad bet. I knew he didn't want me, at least not for more than a few nights, maybe a few weeks, but I let myself believe." It was so stupid on my part. "I'm not the woman that a guy like him falls for, and honestly I don't want to be, but he's kind and sweet. He brought me flowers and asked me to spend time with him and Rosie this week-end. I let myself believe it was more than a kind gesture."

Megan scoffed and slid a worried look at Teddy before she spoke. "You let yourself believe it because he *made* you believe it. Maybe not on purpose, but no man brings a woman flowers if she's just sex to him. He doesn't invite her to go on outings with his kid if he doesn't have feelings for her." She looked at Teddy once again, apology in her green eyes. "I'm sorry but you know it's true."

Teddy lifted her hands up, palms facing out as she shook her head. "You won't get any arguments from me. His actions aren't matching his words, that much is certain."

"Sounds to me like he's feeling things he doesn't want to feel, and trying to convince himself otherwise." Hannah spoke with authority and that grabbed my attention. "Antonio is convinced that he doesn't want or need love after things went sideways with Trishelle. He believes it, but he's not living it."

I rolled my eyes and took another long sip of margarita. "No. I know what you ladies are trying to do and I appreciate it, but it isn't necessary. I made this bed and I am fully capable of getting out of it, washing the sheets and turning the page."

Hannah let out a loud guffaw of laughter and shook her head. "I think you're mixing your metaphors, Gus."

"Doesn't matter. I had a good time with Antonio while it lasted, and I got some really good sex out of it. That's what matters." My dry spell was broken, and I got out just before my heart got broken. "We both got what we wanted out of it."

"Oh god, shut up, please!" Teddy shuddered. "I'll remind you that's my brother you're talking about."

"Yeah, I remember. But he was my lover," I reminded her with a smile.

Teddy gagged and smacked a hand over her ears. "I'm not listening to this."

"Oh, come on, it's not like I'm telling you how well he uses his tongue."

Megan and Hannah laughed gleefully.

Teddy pounded her fist on the table and glared at Hannah. "Is this how you feel when I talk about Cal."

"Yep. Exactly. Well not exactly, because you've actually told me what he does with his tongue." Hannah gave her own shudder and pretended to throw up.

"If that's the case, I'm sorry. So, so sorry." Teddy flashed a sympathetic look at me and sighed. "I'm sorry my brother is a jerk Gus."

"He's not."

"He is," Teddy insisted and refilled my glass. "And we'll keep drinking until you agree."

I accepted the full glass and took a huge gulp, happy and relieved that I didn't have to go through this alone. Pleased that I had people in my life who could and would take care of me when I needed it.

It was more than I ever had before.

Antonio

"**O**h look! There's another princess! Daddy can I take another picture, please?" Rosie bounced up and down with more excitement than one child should be allowed to possess, and tugged on my windbreaker until she had my full attention. "Pretty please, Daddy?"

I looked down at her with a laugh. "I haven't said no yet, why would I start now?" I'd already spent forty bucks just on photos of Rosie and other Renaissance Fair royalty. Queens and Princesses and even a Duchess, all in their best royal finery to match hers.

"Thank you, Daddy!" Rosie took a step back and smiled up at me before she darted off towards the kiosk with Queen Magenta."

"Looks like you made a good pick." Augusta leaned in close, her green eyes focused on Rosie as she spoke animatedly with the queen in pink. "Rosie is just bursting with happiness. Have you ever seen a child so happy?"

"Not this happy," I assured her. "Are you having a good time?"

"I am, actually. It's nice to see a little girl having the time of her life surrounded by people who are just like her, obsessed with royalty. And I can't deny the delight I'll experience later when I get a gargantuan turkey leg."

Her words made me laugh, which made me relax a bit. Augusta was subdued all day, present but not fully. She smiled and laughed in all the right places, but the smile, the laughter, never reached her eyes.

"Gotta love a woman who isn't afraid to eat."

She smiled and shook her head. "Definitely not a problem I have."

I reached for her hand and twined our fingers together until we were palm to palm. "I'm grateful for it. It would be bad form for a chef to be seen with a woman afraid to eat."

Augusta leaned back and arched a reddish-gold brow in my direction. "But we aren't being seen together, so your reputation is perfect intact." The words were right, a little sassy and a little flirty, but they felt...off.

I shrugged. "You never know who's watching."

"Oh, look, Scotch eggs!" She extricated her hand

from mine with such ease that I almost didn't feel the distance between us, but it was there. It was definitely there, I just couldn't figure out why.

By the time I caught up with Augusta, she'd already bought the egg and bit into it with a moan. "Good?"

Her green eyes lit with excitement and pleasure, which only reminded me that it was the first time I'd seen her like that all day. "So good. A little greasy, but in a good way. Want a bite?" When she held the Scotch egg out for me to taste, I grabbed her wrist and kept my eyes on her as I took a bite, slow and sensual.

Her little hitch of breath told me she still wanted me.

I shouldn't have felt so relieved.

But I did.

"Good. Mine are better though. If you play your cards right, I'll make them for you."

She flashed a smile that didn't reach her eyes and said nothing.

It was damned frustrating not to know what she was thinking. A sane man would just ask, but I didn't ask and I couldn't say why. I knew something was wrong, I just didn't know what.

"Oh my gosh, Daddy, Queen Magenta is magical!" Rosie was back with a photo and a wand with a glittery star on the tip. "She can turn fish into fairies and leaves into berries."

"So her village is filled with fairies who smell like fish?"

"Daddy," she giggled sweetly and I couldn't help but smile. "You're silly, Daddy." She spoke around a yawn which meant five hours at the Renaissance Faire was Rosie's limit.

"Daddy is silly, but Rosie is sleepy."

"I'm not," she insisted just as another yawn split her face. "I'm not."

Fighting would only bring on a rare tantrum, so I scooped her in my arms with a grunt. "You know, Rosie, you're almost too big to carry."

"I am a big girl," she shot back, her words slow and sleepy.

"A big girl knows when she's tired and says so ahead of time so she doesn't have to be carried." I hoped she was never too big to let me carry her, but that was my own secret wish.

"I like when you carry me, Daddy." She wrapped her arms around me and smacked a kiss to my cheek. "I just need a nap."

"That's why we're going home, so you can have a nap before dinner."

She gasped in surprise and shot up to look at me. "Tacos?"

"Tacos," I confirmed with a smile.

"Can Nurse Gus come to dinner?"

Hell yes. "If she wants to, she's always welcome to

taco night." I looked at Augusta to let her know I meant what I said. "What do you say to tacos for dinner?"

"That depends. Will there be homemade salsa?"

"Is there any other kind?"

Her face lit with a smile. "Then, I would love to join you and Rosie for dinner. I'll just stop home to wash the fair off me and I'll be there in an hour. Sound good?"

"Sounds perfect."

As soon as we got back to my place, Augusta jumped in her car and took off while I carried Rosie inside and put her down for a nap.

Time in the kitchen was just what I needed after such a confusing afternoon. I started the dough for the taco shells because Rosie preferred the crunch of hard tacos. I tried to figure out what I did to put the distance in Augusta's eyes as I worked. I grabbed a few tomatoes from the basket, an onion and jalapeno pepper and put them on the grill to char them for salsa.

Moving around the kitchen where everything was familiar and I knew just what to do, provided me with immense comfort. It always had. When my grief over losing my mother was too strong, food more than football soothed my pain. Right now, I needed that.

A loud knock sounded at the back door and startled me back to the present. I opened the door with a frown.

"Cal, what the hell? Rosie is sleeping."

My best friend's worried gaze put me on edge and when he raked a hand through his hair, I took a step back. "Do you ever answer your damn phone?"

I patted my pockets at his words and groaned. "Shit, I think it's in the car. What's wrong?"

"Man, there are photos of you and Trishelle all over the internet, wondering if you had a secret getaway in NYC to talk about getting back together."

"Bullshit. She ambushed me on the street with her little cameras hidden. We are *not* getting back together. Ever."

"I believe you, man. But if the photos reached me, don't you think they'll get to Gus? And your dad? And the rest of Jackson's Ridge?"

Shit. "I knew she was up to something, but after all this time, I figured she would just forget about it."

Cal let out a loud bark of laughter. "You thought your fame-hungry ex-wife would just forget about a juicy second chance story line? I don't know if that was wishful thinking on your part or willful naïveté."

"No, Cal, don't hold back. Tell me what you really think."

"Gladly. I think you better call Gus right now and explain to her before she sees those photos."

Augusta. "Shit." I patted my pockets for my phone and cursed again. "Give me your phone."

Cal handed it over with a sympathetic smile. "Good luck."

She answered on the first ring. "What's up, Cal?"

"It's Antonio. Don't hang up." The phone call ended before the request was even out of my mouth. "She hung up."

Cal let out a low whistle and shook his head. "I'm sorry, man. Let her cool down and then explain what happened. Gus is a reasonable woman, just give her time."

I glanced at the clock on the oven and sighed. "She's supposed to be coming for dinner in less than an hour."

"Oh. I'll stay until then if you want?"

I nodded. "Thanks man." I shook my head as I washed and breaded the fish for tacos. "She won't understand."

"She might."

I looked up at my best friend. "Seriously?"

Cal shrugged. "Teddy thinks she'll be pissed you didn't tell her when you came back from New York."

"I told Trishelle I wouldn't sign a release form, and I figured she couldn't use the footage."

"Ah. You figured you wouldn't have to tell anyone about it, specifically Augusta. Why?"

"Because I was trying to avoid *this*." I shook my head. Augusta, if she showed up, would be angry, maybe hurt. "This is exactly why I don't like to get involved."

Getting involved with a woman always came with complications and I told myself I was done with that when I left Trishelle.

"You're not involved," Cal shot back with a shrug and a knowing smile. "You said she knew the score, which means you're not involved."

Yeah I said that, but now I wasn't so sure. "Cal," I groaned.

"What? Those were your words. Right?"

"Yeah, I said it but I'm not sure if that was the truth." There, I admitted it. "I like Augusta. I like spending time with her, cooking for her and sleeping with her. But...hell, man, I don't know."

Cal huffed out a laugh. "We never know, that's what makes love so scary."

"It's not love," I growled.

Cal ignored me. "How do you think I felt, knowing that I was falling for my best friend's sister? I couldn't do a damn thing about how I felt for Teddy, even knowing that it might ruin our friendship."

"I said it's not love."

"Maybe it is, maybe it isn't. The point is, you're worried about how Gus will react to those photos which means you give a damn."

"Of course, I give a damn. She's great and I don't want to hurt her." Gus didn't deserve to get caught up with the drama my ex-wife created.

Cal sighed and stood just as the doorbell rang.

"That's a good place to start. I'll call you later. Good luck." He slipped out the back door while I went to open the front door for Augusta.

I smiled at the sight she made in a denim skirt and a green V-neck t-shirt. It was a modest outfit, cute rather than sexy. "Augusta. You look beautiful. Come in." I leaned forward to greet her with a kiss and she ducked away from me.

"I'm here because Rosie invited me and I don't want to let her down. That's the *only* reason I'm here."

My shoulders fell in disappointment. This wouldn't be easy. "I'm sorry, Augusta."

She stepped inside, careful not to touch me, and shook her head. "I don't need an apology, Antonio. I know the score." Her green eyes pierced a hole into me until realization dawned.

She heard me at The Outpost. "That was out of context," I tried to explain. "The guys were giving me a hard time and I was trying to make them stop."

"At my expense? Got it."

Okay, that didn't help. "No, not at your expense. I just didn't want to talk about it, hell I had no idea what to say about it."

Augusta held up a hand and shook her head. "It's fine, Antonio. I knew you weren't serious about me, and you were quite clear that wasn't part of your plan and I still slept with you. No hard feelings."

"No hard feelings? You sound angry and you hung up on me earlier."

"Fine," she spat out. "There *are* some hard feelings, but not because I expected you to fall in love with me or for this to turn into something more than a fling. I'm upset because, it doesn't matter. I am upset now, but I won't be for much longer." She wrapped her arms around herself as if she needed to protect herself from me, and watching that was like a drop-kick to the gut. "I just wish you would have told me."

Now I was angry. "So you just believe everything you read, Augusta? You don't even want to hear my side of the story?"

She shook her head, red tendrils falling from the messy bun she wore on top of her head. "I didn't need to read any story, Antonio, I have eyes. I saw how close you were standing, the heat as you gazed down at her. I'm not blind and I'm not stupid. You loved her enough to marry her and have a kid with her, it's a connection that won't ever be severed."

"She severed it when she almost let my daughter die so she could feed her addiction!" I shook my head and took a step forward. "Trishelle is the last woman on earth I would ever sleep with, never mind while I'm already sleeping with someone else."

She nodded and the tension in her shoulders faded, a little. "I believe you, but it doesn't matter."

"It does matter, dammit. Trishelle ambushed me on

the street, set this little meeting up for her stupid, fucking show and you're going to let it come between us? You're gonna let her come between us? Un-fucking-believable."

Augusta smiled, it was sweet but sad, and tore at my heart. "It isn't your ex-wife coming between us, Antonio. It's us. You were never going to be serious about me and it's probably best that this all happened now, because I'm not sure I could sleep with you for much longer without falling for you." She sighed as if just saying those words were like a weight off her shoulders. "So you see, you don't need to feel guilty about being with your ex. I won't hold it against you."

"Daddy! Daddy! Did you make the tacos?" Rosie barreled down the stairs full of energy after her nap, unaware of the tension between the adults. "Nurse Gus, you're here!"

Augusta smiled down at Rosie's wide grin. "I am, and I was expecting to eat dinner with the Taco Princess."

Rosie turned wide eyes up to me. "Is that a thing?"

I shrugged. "You're a princess, you can make it a thing can't you?"

My daughter gasped and her excited eyes bounced between me and Augusta. "Be right back!"

"Taco Princess," I repeated with a smile. "I'm curious to see what she comes up with."

"Me too," Augusta agreed, her words quiet and sad.

She sat through dinner, indulging Rosie's questions about her life as a nurse while we ate our fill of fish tacos, fresh chips, salsa, and cheese dip. Sadness filled her eyes and she barely looked at me through the meal.

When she finally walked away and left me with a sad smile, I realized just how much Augusta meant to me.

Damn.

Gus

✿

I don't care. That was my mantra for the past day or two. I don't give a damn. Not about the fact that Antonio got cozy with his ex-wife while he was in New York and then came home to me, and yeah, gave me some of the best orgasms of my life. Not about any of it.

Okay, I cared, but I wouldn't care for much longer.

Antonio was a temporary lover and that was it. There were no promises that existed between us, other than the promise of mutual pleasure. And that was just fine by me.

Totally fine.

I slapped on a happy face as I clocked in for my shift, hoping that my canary yellow scrubs would brighten my gloomy disposition. The pediatric patients needed me and I wouldn't let them down, no matter the mess of my personal life.

"Are you all right, Gus?" Melanie's voice pulled me from my thoughts and I looked up with a smile I didn't feel.

"Of course. I'm fine," I assured her. Fine was my default state. No matter what happened in my life, maternal abandonment, paternal alcoholism, I was always fine. Always. No gorgeous bad boy with a hard-on for his ex-wife would change that. "Why do you ask?"

"Your eyes seem sad." Melanie tipped her head to the side as she studied me, a clear sign she didn't believe that I was fine. I just hoped she didn't want to talk about it.

"I think it's just exhaustion," I assured her with a half-hearted grin.

"You sure?"

"Completely."

"Because it could be all the lies about Antonio and his skank of an ex-wife. You do know it's all lies, don't you?" She shook her head. "They lie about everything just to get you to buy a magazine or click an article. You can't believe a word of it."

That much was true, but I also couldn't believe in the word of a man. A mortal man. "Sure."

Melanie shook her head and let out a long, frustrated sigh. "Honey, it's okay to be sad. It's okay to be angry about what you saw online."

I nodded. "It is okay, and if I felt anything, I'd be fine with it. But I don't."

Melanie shrugged. "All right. If you need to vent or to talk, I'm here."

"Thanks, Mel. I need to start my shift now but if I get the urge to talk, I'll find you." It was time to get to work, it was just what I needed to think about anything but Antonio and his ex-wife. They were irrelevant to my life as it was today. I got what I needed from Antonio and now it was time to move on.

"You better." Her sing-song voice put a smile on my face as I made my way to the pediatric wing of the medical center.

The kids were all in good spirits, and the first few hours of my shift flew by in a haze of charts and conversations about the best toys and cartoons and teen dramas. The day was no different than any other shift, and soon enough, I found that my smiles didn't require effort, my laughter came easily. I didn't have to try to enjoy my shift, I just did.

As the day progressed, I felt myself start to feel better. There was more energy in my step, more volume in my laughter and more swing in my hips. I was still upset about Antonio, but I refused to let it impact my entire day. That's what I told myself because it helped.

Because that's what I needed to get through another round of disappointment.

That's all it was, disappointment. I wasn't heartbroken that things hadn't worked out with Antonio, I was disappointed, mostly in myself for succumbing to dreams over reality.

"Augusta, there you are." Suzie's sharp voice broke into my thoughts and I looked up from a chart to find her marching towards me, purpose in her steps.

"Here I am, Suzie. What's up?" I braced myself for her judgment or advice. Everyone I'd run into today had offered one or the other.

Suzie pushed her glasses up on her nose and sighed. "I just wanted you to know that men are men, and their wants and needs can shift with the wind. One minute they know exactly what they want in a woman and the next, they only know what they don't want. They are confounding creatures, and we only put up with them because they have muscles and smell good. Really damn good."

I smiled as Suzie got carried away by her own thoughts. "Thanks, Suzie, but that's nothing I need to concern myself with. What Antonio does with his wife is none of my business." I took my time making rounds, giving each patient my full attention until everyone had been seen, every chart had been updated.

I was on my way to the nurse's lounge when my

back pocket vibrated with a text message. Antonio. "It's not what you think."

I had to give the man credit for his persistence. He wasn't one to give up without a fight, which would have been admirable if he wasn't doing it to prove he was a good guy. I ignored the message for a few hours until my shift was over because I refused to be one of the nurses crying her eyes out in the lounge, while making sure the entire hospital knew about my miserable love life.

No, thank you.

When my shift was over and I could ease the tightness in my shoulders a little, I decided to answer Antonio. "You don't owe me an explanation. But, thank you for your concern." That was mature and to the point. Right? I didn't expect a response, so I shoved the phone back into my pocket and headed towards the exit.

Ten hours wasn't long enough to get over whatever it was I needed to get over where Antonio was concerned, but it was enough for me to push him out of my mind a little bit more. On the way home, Hannah called.

"I'm fine Hannah."

"Good," she laughed. "That means you won't have to think up an excuse to get out of coming out for drinks with me tonight."

Drinks? "Sure, that would be great actually."

Hannah and I didn't hang out much, but she was a friend and I could use some company tonight. "Meet in an hour?"

"Nah, I don't want to give you a chance to back out. I'll be at your place in thirty." She ended the call before I could say another word.

Smart woman.

I made a quick call to invite Suzie and rushed through the front door hoping to squeeze in a quick shower. But Hannah showed up sooner than I expected.

"Don't worry about me, I'll just make myself comfortable while you make yourself presentable."

The laughter in her voice put a smile on my face. I dressed quickly after the shower, in jeans and a pretty tunic that was light and airy against the unusually warm evening. "Ready."

"You look good." Hannah stood with a warm smile. "Let's go."

The Outpost was busier than usual, then again it had been a long time since I was there on any night but a Friday. My stomach growled as soon as we grabbed a big table near the front corner of the bar. "I think I'll have some fried mushrooms."

"That sounds great," Teddy shouted when she dropped down in a chair. "Add some mozzarella sticks to the order too. I'm starved." How she could put away so many calories and stay so slender, I'd never know. But I wish I knew her secret.

"I don't know how you eat that," Megan told her with a shake of her head. "I just gained three pounds listening to you wax poetically about it."

"Oh sure," Suzie snorted. "The baker with the ass that won't quit is whining about fried foods. Give me a break."

I laughed and wrapped an arm around Suzie. "I appreciate your candor."

"Thanks," she grinned. "I'll pretend you're not even a little tipsy."

"Thanks back," I told her with a wide, overly bright grin. It was nice to be surrounded by friends again, especially after everything with Antonio. It helped me forget that I wasn't enough for him, that I was never enough. The alcohol and the friendship made it easier to forget that he had been so dissatisfied with me, or maybe my performance, that he called up his ex the moment the wheels touched down in New York.

It was no coincidence they'd ended up in New York at the same time. It couldn't be. Could it?

No matter. We hadn't crossed paths much since he moved back to Jackson's Ridge, and since we didn't travel in the same social circles, it was safe to say we wouldn't in the future.

Then he showed up with Cal, and I let out a groan that was slightly louder than I meant it to be. Maybe I was a little bit tipsy. He was with Cal, so there was no doubt they would end up at my table.

Teddy turned in the direction of my gaze and sighed. "Sorry." She didn't look sorry, just like a woman in love who was happy to see her man.

"It's fine. I should get going anyway." If I could just slide from the booth, I could make a quick getaway with nothing more than a hello. I fixed a bland smile on my face and pushed out of the booth, and right into the wide familiar chest of Antonio. "Excuse me." I didn't look up, I knew it was him by his scent, the hard muscles that lined his chest and abs.

"Going somewhere?"

"Yeah. Home." I tried to go around him, but Antonio was feeling playful, stepping in front of me no matter which way I tried to go. "Antonio," I sighed. "Stop."

"Stop, what?" He flashed a grin that, yeah, was a panty-melter. Too bad for him, because he did nothing for me. Not anymore.

"Stop this, whatever you're doing." At the sudden silence around the table, I closed my eyes and sighed, because we had the full attention of everyone. "This is unnecessary."

"Not to me." His tone was serious, almost sincere, and if I hadn't heard him dismiss me so unequivocally, and if I hadn't seen the look in his eyes when he stared at his ex, I might have believed him.

Not tonight. "That sounds like a personal problem."

"It's very fucking personal," he growled back. "Just admit that you're mad or hurt or whatever and we can move forward." Of course he thought that. He could flash that smile and flex those biceps while he offered up a half-hearted apology and women probably swooned, took him at his word.

I already did that once. "I'm not mad, and even if I was, I would have no right to be, Antonio. We were nothing, just a fling, right? Temporary lovers who owe each other nothing." Less than nothing, in fact.

"Ouch." Teddy's attempt at a whisper failed miserably, causing a low hum of laughter from the table.

"You know that's not true," he insisted and stepped in closer with a hand on my shoulder. "We talked. We connected."

I shrugged off his touch. "I know the score, Antonio. At least I do now."

He turned to Cal for help, but his friend shrugged as if to say, "Leave me out of it."

"I heard you say it and you know what? I gave you the benefit of the doubt and showed up for the Renaissance Fair with you and Rosie. Then I found out you were meeting up with your ex."

"I wasn't meeting up with her," he growled. "I told you she ambushed me."

"Totally a move Trishelle would make," Teddy

confirmed. "What?" she asked when I glared her. "It's true. She's a total schemer."

I shook my head. "It doesn't matter. You have a connection, a history with her and you didn't tell me about it for a reason. Because I had no right to know, because we aren't anything."

"Oh, good point," Hannah offered like the official scorekeeper of this little...whatever it was.

"It's not a good point," he shot back to Hannah, but his angry, pleading gaze never left mine. "I would never get back with Trishelle Augusta, and you know why."

"I know that's what you think." This wouldn't be the first time that I was cast in the role of *the reason another couple reconciles*.

"She's got a new reality show and she's trying to push the storyline of us getting back together. It's all about the screen time for her." He pulled me close and resisted my efforts to break free of his hold.

"I know what I saw, and you didn't look like a reluctant participant, Antonio. And even if you did, it's none of my damn business." That's what the photos had highlighted for me, that he didn't give me a heads up that his meeting with his ex might become public, was because I didn't need to know.

"Stop saying that!"

I shrugged. "The truth hurts, believe me I know. But now that I do, I get it. I understand." I leaned into him, into his heat, for only a moment, just long enough for his grip to slacken. With a pat to his hard chest, I took a step back and shook my head. "No hard feelings." I walked away, because I had to. I needed to get away from the weight of his stare on me. I needed to get away from the expectations at the table. It was impossible not to feel for Antonio, but I refused to be the bad guy in this situation.

There was no good or bad guy, just two people who's time together had expired.

The chilly night air hit my skin and I let out a long, slow breath. Confrontation wasn't my strong suit except at work. In my scrubs, I would defend a child's treatment plan until I was breathless, no matter how many parents were offended or angry. In my personal life, I found it easier to just walk away. Experience had thought me that. When it had become clear that Dad wouldn't stop drinking, not for anything, I'd had to save myself.

"No hard feelings? What in the hell is that supposed to mean?" Antonio's angry growl hit me right in the back and that moment of relaxation felt like a lifetime ago.

I stopped and dropped my head and shoulders in resignation. This conversation would happen whether I wanted it to or not. Again. "It means that I have no hard feelings about being with you or how things ended."

"Then things don't have to end between us." The plea in his voice almost got to me. Almost.

"They already have ended, Antonio, if there was anything to end."

"There was," he growled and suddenly he was at my side, his hand gripped the upper part of my arm and spun me towards him. "We have something, dammit. It might be casual, but it is something, something important, at least to me."

"If that were true, you would have been honest about what happened in New York. You kept it to yourself, you hid it for a reason."

"I didn't hide it. I didn't bring it up because I didn't sign a release form which means they can't use the footage for the show."

"Right. Or maybe you were hedging your bets, Antonio. Maybe you want your ex more than you care to admit. Or maybe you just don't want to admit the truth, that you didn't tell me because I didn't need to know. You never promised me anything and I never asked you to, so why are you making this so damn difficult?"

"I don't know," he answered honestly, his tone barely above a whisper. "I just want you to know, that what you saw online was nothing."

"Duly noted." I turned to walk away, but his grip remained firm. Tight. "Antonio," I growled, because I needed to get away. The urge to run was strong, almost overwhelming.

"Augusta," he growled back and crushed his mouth to mine. The kiss wasn't just any old kiss, not even from the start. His mouth was strong and demanding, his tongue slicked back and forth across my top lip, my bottom lip, teasing the seam of my mouth until it opened up and allowed him entry.

Antonio's kiss was like a drug, no matter how bad it was, how addictive, how destructive, you couldn't deny it. Couldn't stay away. My body melted into his, right in the middle of The Outpost parking lot. He accepted my weight, one hand gripped my hip while the other cupped my face. He held me like I mattered, like I was truly important to him and he kissed me with a wild, feverish abandon that spoke of pure lust.

White hot, fiery lust that pulled me closer and closer to the flame until it surrounded us. The heat licked at my skin, or maybe that was just the impact of being in Antonio's arms, being the sole target of his mouth and his hands.

I clawed at him and he gripped me tighter, pulled me closer. If we didn't slow down soon, we would be naked and writhing, panting and pleasing each other. In public.

The kiss was hot as hell and I couldn't deny the effect it had on me. I was hot and bothered, turned on and ready to make another mistake. Another mistake that might put my heart, my well-being, in danger.

Danger.

Antonio was dangerous to my heart.

I pulled back and sighed, my fingers touched my lips, swollen from the ferocity of his kiss. I couldn't do this with him. No matter how good it felt, I couldn't. "Good night, Antonio." I walked away because I had to, but that didn't mean it was easy. It wasn't, and I spent the short walk home in a haze.

Antonio

✿

"Daddy, do you think Nurse Gus will like my dress?" Rosie looked down at her sparkly purple dress with her purple sneakers that Hannah had bedazzled and then back up at me with worry in her eyes.

I lifted her from my truck and set her on the ground in the medical center parking lot. Rosie put her hand in mine and waited for my answer. "I think she'll not only like it, she might be jealous that she doesn't have a dress just like it."

Rosie giggled. "Nurses can't wear princess dresses, Daddy." She shook her head as we entered the medical center, smiling and chatting with everyone she encountered like she was mayor of Jackson's Ridge.

"How do you know they can't wear dresses?"

She shrugged and stepped inside the elevator. "If they could, all the nurses would wear 'em."

Who was I to argue with that logic? "I stand corrected."

Rosie chatted with a little girl in the waiting room while I checked in, my gaze scanned the floor in search of familiar red hair, usually in a topknot or a ponytail. Augusta. She would be here today, I knew that. What I didn't know, was how she would react to me.

"Have a seat," the unfamiliar nurse smiled. "You know the drill."

"Too well," I shot back and took a seat that allowed me to keep an eye on Rosie. And on the lookout for Augusta.

Eventually, the door opened and Augusta appeared. "Rosie."

"That's me. I'm here!" Rosie darted out of her seat and ran towards Augusta, barreling into her for a warm hug. "Hi, Nurse Gus."

"Hello Princess Rosie, how are you feeling today?"

"I'm good. Do you like my dress?" She spun excitedly until the skirt of her dress flared out.

"I love it. Purple is definitely your color. Are we ready to go back?" Her gaze slid to mine quickly before she turned her attention back to Rosie.

"Yep." Rosie grabbed her hand and the two females disappeared down the hall, and I had to catch up or get left behind.

Augusta chatted with Rosie, took her vitals, and ignored me unless she needed to ask a question. "Any attacks? Breathing problems outside the norm?"

"None that she's reported to me."

"All right. The doctor will be with you shortly. It was good to see you today, Your Royal Highness."

Rosie giggled. "You too, Nurse Gus. I missed you."

Augusta's smile faltered at my daughter's words. "I missed you too, but I'm happy that you don't need to come so often anymore. It means you're getting better." It was an impressive dodge.

I followed her from the exam room, determined to get her to talk to me. Hell, to even just look at me. "You said no hard feelings, but you won't even talk to me."

In response, she kept her gaze on Rosie's chart. "This is how things were between us before we got naked together, Antonio. You're just upset that I'm no longer a nervous, swooning mess in your presence."

Her words put a smile on my face. "I did like seeing you flustered, and it turned me on knowing I was the reason why."

She almost looked up from the chart when she pointed behind her. "There are plenty of women in the nurse's lounge who will give your ego the boost it so dearly needs."

A rumbling laugh exploded out of me. No woman but Teddy called me on my bullshit the way Augusta did. "Maybe so, Augusta, but none of those women are you."

She rolled her eyes at my words. "Exactly."

"Augusta, come on. We can be friends, can't we?"

She shook her head and finally settled those green eyes on me. "No, we can't. We weren't friends before and I see no reason to change that."

"We know each other now."

She shook her head. "We know things about each other now, that's all."

I folded my arms and stared at her. "So there are hard feelings?"

"No," she sighed. "I just don't see a reason to add more complications when we could just go back to how things were before."

"But I didn't know you then and I do now. I want to know more of you, Augusta."

"No, you don't." Her laugh wasn't mean-spirited or bitter, it was more condescending that anything. "I'm nothing special, Antonio."

"That's where you're wrong, Augusta. You are more special than you know."

"And I don't need your pretty, complimentary words. Save them for your next woman, okay?"

I blinked innocently. "That's what I'm doing."

Finally, her face split into a reluctant smile. "I'll see you around, Antonio." The sway of her hips tempted, the swing of her ass covered in deep red scrubs teased as she marched away from me, determined to put as much space between us as possible.

That was too bad because she was all I thought about since that kiss in the parking lot. That hot as hell kiss that said she still wanted me.

Which gave me something to work with.

Gus

❧

"What a long day," I said to no one in particular as I pulled the dirty, puke-covered scrubs from my locker and shoved them into my backpack to be washed when I got home, which would be soon thankfully. The day felt like three shifts rolled into one, especially after Antonio and Rosie's visit. The little girl was as adorable as she always was, but Antonio, he was determined.

The question was why.

Why did he want to talk to me now that I'd given him the casual fling he wanted? It didn't make any sense, and I spent most of my shift trying to suss out his motives, and I came up empty.

Worrying about Antonio wasn't a productive use of my time. Getting home safely and quickly, that was how I planned to spend the next fifteen minutes before I fell into a deep sleep.

"Ah, there you are Gus!" Melanie popped her head in with the friendly smile she wore when she was about to ask a favor. "How's it going?" Her gaze dropped from my face to my bag.

"Good. I'm getting ready to go home. What's up, Mel?"

She stepped inside with a sigh. "Two of the ER nurses called in, down with the flu."

"Again?" A few weeks ago a bug had taken out half the ER.

"Oh please," Melanie rolled her eyes. "This is the Reardon Black Project flu. He's performing tonight at the Pavilion and they think I don't know it," she snorted and shook her head. "Like I don't want to see that handsome fella shake his tush while tickling those guitar strings."

Her words brought a smile to my tired face. Melanie was a character, plain spoken and honest to a fault. "Why don't you go?"

"Because someone has to run this place, don't they? Besides, I have plans tonight. At home plans," she clarified unnecessarily. "So, can you work tonight?"

I wanted to say no. I was exhausted and in no mood to socialize for another ten hours, but I couldn't leave the ER short-handed. They needed help and I could provide it. My gift and my curse. "Yeah, I can."

She perked up. "Thanks, Gus! I can always count on you." Melanie meant the words to be a compliment, I knew that, but today they didn't feel like one.

"That's me, good ol' reliable Gus." Where had being steady and reliable gotten me in life? *A good job and a wonderful circle of friends?* Damn my stupid subconscious, who asked her anyway?

"That's not a bad thing, Gus. Don't let anyone make you feel otherwise."

"Thanks, Mel." I said the words even though I didn't mean them, and changed into a pair of clean scrubs that were a size too small. Everywhere. A quick splash of cold water on my face woke me up and I found an elastic band to wrap around my thick hair. I was as ready as I would be for another double shift.

Cal worked the ER and I found him right out front, staring down at a chart. "Hey Gus, thanks for covering tonight. You're my favorite fill in." He flashed his patented smile but it did nothing to take the sting off his unintended slight.

I kept my bland smile in place and shrugged. "Story of my life."

Cal's smile disappeared and he reached out to me, a frown appeared when I stepped back. "I didn't mean it like that."

I held up a hand to stop his unnecessary apology. "I know. Don't worry about it. Where do you need me?"

He still wore a horrified look that made me slightly

uncomfortable, but I waited him out. I wouldn't apologize for how I felt. "Um..."

"MVA, incoming! Internal injuries, lacerations and a broken leg." Mel's voice boomed and Cal and I got moving, him towards the ambulance bay while I went to prep what he would need in the OR.

The next few hours passed in a blur of emergency medical needs, from a drunken prank that resulted in a split open hand, several broken limbs that belonged to daredevil kids, and a domestic abuse case that resulted in broken ribs. I hated to see the way people were so casual about their safety. Hated to see them bloody and broken.

But it was the distraction I needed. The perfect bloody, broken mess to keep my mind on the patient in front of me, not a dark haired, dark eyed bad boy who was no good for me. I spent too many years trying to get a man to love me, and he'd chosen the bottle every single time.

I was done with that life.

Totally done.

"Nothing like an almost full moon to make a shift fly by." Cal shook his head and let out a sigh as he stretched his back and neck. "Ready to hit the break room?"

I was ready to hit my pillow, but I still had five hours to go before that became a reality. "Nah, I already ate the lunch I brought earlier so I'm headed to the cafeteria. I'll catch up with you after."

He shook his head and reached for my arm. "Nope. We're going to the break room." He tugged me down the corridor until we stood in front of the blue door, and pushed it open with an odd flourish. The drab, utilitarian break room with a wide circular table in the middle looked like it had this morning, except for the food piled on the table.

"What's all this?" The question was rhetorical because I knew the answer. I made this same char Siu a few weeks ago. The platter was decorated with more precision and everything was done much better than my efforts, but it was undeniable. "Cal, tell me you didn't set this up."

When I turned to Cal, he held his hands up defensively and shook his head. "All I did was mention to Antonio that you'd been roped into a double shift. This was all him."

I didn't believe that for a moment, but Antonio was his best friend and he wouldn't speak ill of him. That was fine, I didn't want him to. "I'm just going to have a salad. You and the rest of the ER department should enjoy it, though." Not only did I not want to appreciate this gesture from Antonio, I had a fried chicken sandwich from Dad for lunch and I needed something healthy, something with vegetables.

Cal stood in front of the door with his arms folded

across his chest, a scowl on his face. "Sit down and eat or I'll lock us both in here for the next thirty minutes." His brows arched in amusement. "That will get the hospital tags wagging which might lead Teddy to kick your ass. That might be kind of hot though, so I'm good either way."

"Gross," I groaned and dropped into one of the empty seats. "This is ridiculous." The food smelled incredible, the sauce made my mouth water and I looked at the table with longing. Crispy pork with noodles, Asian slaw, dumplings and three different dipping sauces.

"Eat," he ordered while he piled his plate high with food.

I made a plate of my own because Antonio was a damn good cook and it was no hardship to eat his food. I told myself it was a no-strings attached meal. Eating it didn't obligate me to more. "So good."

"He's not a bad guy, you know."

And here we go. Stuck in a room with his best friend to help plead his case. "I know that, and I never said he was." I reached for a dumpling and took my time while Cal stared at me as he shoveled food in his face. "Antonio covets his bachelor status even more than you did, and I'm not looking to change that."

Cal nodded and adjusted the chopsticks in his hand. "I did covet my status but once I realized how much

Teddy meant to me, it wasn't even a question of whether I'd change my status for her. It was a given."

"That's sweet." Teddy was a lucky woman to have a man who loved her and wasn't afraid to admit it.

"It's also true." He flashed a wide, knowing grin and his eyes softened at the mention of his woman.

"It's clear to anyone with eyes that you love Teddy, but I'm not that woman for Antonio and I'm okay with that. But what I'm not okay with, is being his bit of fun while he finds that woman."

"You think that's what you are?"

I nodded. "I know I am. We had fun together, a lot of fun. But it was only fun."

"I don't know, Gus. I've known Antonio my whole life and he's not the big gesture kind of guy, not even for Trishelle. This is a pretty big gesture."

"Oh please." I rolled my eyes. "Not too hard to figure out that the chubby girl would appreciate a meal cooked by a professional."

"That's not how he sees you, trust me." Cal's expression was intense, his defense of his best friend, unflinching. "You mean something to him, Gus."

I tried to shrug off those words ,because warmth spread through my body the moment they hit my ears. I wanted to believe that, but it wasn't the truth.

"I don't, Cal. I've been here before and I know that I don't. This is all because his ego is bruised because I walked away before he could."

Antonio

With Rosie at the community center for a few hours, I used the time to myself to create next month's production schedule. Not exactly what the world expected of the Bad Boy Chef, but this was reality. Production schedules, vacuuming and picking up tiaras and tulle. And yeah, I now knew what the hell tulle actually was, or as Rosie called it, fluffy princess dress material.

Movement came from the porch and provided the perfect distraction from the half-empty production schedule that mocked me for the past thirty minutes. I crept to the front door, expecting to see mischievous teenagers ready to ring my bell and run, or a flaming bag of crap on my doormat. What I wasn't expecting was a mass of auburn waves bent over my step while familiar hands arranged a pile of plastic food containers.

Augusta.

She looked up and gasped, clearly she hadn't expected to see me. More like she wanted to avoid it. "You could have rung the bell, Augusta."

With a sigh, she put her hands to her thighs and stood. "I didn't want to disturb you, but these needed to be returned to you. Thank you for the food, it was a nice gesture."

Nice. I snorted at that word, at her chilly reception. "Nice? My goal was to remind you of my good qualities." I wondered if she still believed I had any.

"Well you are an excellent chef," she said with a half-watt smile. "And a pretty good teacher." Her words were sincere but they contained no warmth.

"Glad you agree." I took a step back and motioned for her to come inside, a move that risked rejection, but I needed alone time with her.

Augusta shook her head and tucked a lock of her hair behind her ear, a nervous gesture. "No thanks. I've got plans."

I gave her a skeptical look. "Part of those plans included returning my containers?"

She nodded, her expression wary.

"They haven't actually been returned yet." I smiled at her low growl.

"Whatever." She squatted down and scooped up the

half dozen containers and marched inside, reluctance obvious with every step. I followed the sway of her hips until they came to a stop in my kitchen. She set them down and whirled around, annoyance threading her brows into a deep vee. "Happy?"

Hell no, I wasn't happy. Not with the way she was determined to treat me like a stranger, as if I didn't know the way she felt wrapped around my cock, the way her whole body flushed right before she reached orgasm. As if I didn't know the way she tasted. I needed to think. Fast.

"No, I'm not."

"Antonio." She said my name on a long sigh and shook her head. "Your containers have been returned and I'm grateful for the food. Let's just leave it at that, all right?"

Like I could do that even if I wanted to. "No, Augusta, it's not all right. I need a recipe tester and you're here, *and* you think I'm a fantastic chef."

"Teddy is your recipe tester. Everyone knows that."

I nodded. "Except she's still snuggled in bed with Cal, which I don't want to think about, and most importantly, she's not here. She should have been here an hour ago, I don't think she's gonna show today. So basically my production schedule is screwed if you don't help me out."

"Oh."

It was a dick move to play on her guilt, but until she

softened towards me I would take what I could get. "Yeah. So?"

She shook her head and red waves cascaded around her shoulders, making my fingers itch to touch her. "Sorry to hear that. Good luck." She skirted around me and left the kitchen, making a beeline for the front door.

"You could do it." Just as I expected, my words stopped the fast movement of her feet.

"I can't. Plans."

Stubborn woman. "With?"

The tension was back in her shoulders. "None of your business."

I laughed at the fire in her voice. "Afraid I'm going to scare him away?"

"Hardly," she snorted. "I don't think you could pull off jealousy if you tried. And Megan doesn't scare easily."

It wasn't a date, and that was something I could work with. I reached for my phone with a smile, knowing this move put my jewels and my life, at risk. "Megan, hey. It's Antonio." Augusta turned around with a shocked scowl.

"Antonio. What are you up to?" Not exactly the bubbly greeting I usually got, but I could handle it.

"Great to hear your voice too. Listen, do you mind if Augusta takes a rain-check for meeting up with you today? She really wants to stay and test some new recipes for me but she doesn't want to leave you hanging."

"That is a bold-faced lie," Augusta shouted from the door, her sneaker-clad feet brought her back to the kitchen. She growled again when I winked at her.

Megan sighed on the phone. "I don't know what the hell you're up to, but if you can get her to stay, then no, I don't mind."

"Excellent! Thanks, Megan. I'll let Augusta know that you don't mind. At all."

She laughed. "Tell her to call me later for bail money, or a shovel and tarp."

I stumbled over my words, slightly. "Um, yeah, will do."

"Good luck."

If those were Megan's expectations for the afternoon, I might need more than luck. "She said call her later and tell her all about it."

"Liar. Let's hope I need bail and not a shovel." Augusta folded her arms, a move that brought her cleavage front and center, and arched a brow as she looked around the kitchen. "Doesn't look like you've started cooking anything."

Busted. "Why bother when Teddy didn't answer her phone?"

"Bull. I'm not doing this with you, Antonio. Go play your games somewhere else."

"IT's not a game," I growled. "It's my work. My career. This is how I take care of my kid."

She waved off my words. "Don't give me that crap, you know exactly what I mean. This little ploy is a game, not your work." Augusta shook her head. "What is the point of all this, Antonio?"

"Other than Teddy, you're the most honest with me and I need that." It was the truth, even if it was only a part of it. I didn't know why I was acting this way, couldn't figure out my own damn motives. Mostly. "I just like being around you, Augusta."

"No, you like sleeping with me, and we're not doing that anymore."

"A travesty," I sighed sadly. "But even with your clothes on, I like being around you Augusta."

My words caught her off guard and tension stiffened her body while she thought about my request. It was hard for most people to pass up the type of food I cooked for my channel, I saved the real show stoppers for my subscribers, but I let her take her time to think it through. No pressure. No persuasion. I knew I had her when her shoulders relaxed ever so slightly.

"Fine. You get two hours, Antonio. No more."

"Three. I still have to set up lights and the camera."

She folded her arms. "Two."

It wasn't nearly enough, but it was a good start. "I'll take it."

Gus

"That was easy." Too easy, in fact. Antonio was up to something, and I didn't know what. "Why?"

He shrugged and flashed that flirty smile that turned my insides to mashed potatoes. "Arguing with you would get me nowhere, but my food can tempt you to stay." He moved around the kitchen to set up lights and position the camera while he spoke. "That's my true super power."

Maybe. "Two hours," I repeated for my benefit as much as Antonio's. This was me being neighborly, nothing more. "What will I be tasting?"

Something dirty was on the tip of his tongue, I could see the mischief in his eyes, but he managed to keep it to himself. "The episode is From Everyday to Gourmet."

"Catchy." I winced at the sarcasm in my tone. Bitchy wasn't my default, but damn him, Antonio had cornered me by calling Megan and laying a massive guilt trip on me. I had no choice but to stay. To help.

As if he actually needed my help.

"Thanks," he replied completely unaffected by my tone. "I thought so too." He leaned across the counter between us until there was less than six inches of space between his face and mine, rested his chin in his hand so that his sun-kissed, tattooed forearms were on display. Tempting me. "So, Augusta, tell me. What's your favorite thing to eat when you're too tired to be creative?"

Good question. "Easy. Mac & cheese."

He shuddered, his dark eyes horrified. "Not the powder stuff, I hope?"

I frowned, offended. "No. I am a real life adult, Antonio."

He licked his lips, my gaze watched his pink tongue slide back and forth across his bottom lip and then the top lip. *Holy hell.* "Oh, alright." He pushed back with a smile and another wink. "We'll start with mac & cheese then."

My brows furrowed in suspicion. "I thought you already had a shoot scheduled for today?"

He frowned in response, feigning confusion. "Did I say that?"

"Antonio," I growled and pushed away from the counter. "No more games."

"None, I swear." He turned and moved around the kitchen gracefully, like a choreographed dancer while he grabbed what seemed like dozens of ingredients. When he finally stopped moving, he stood between two sets of ingredients.

I let out a low whistle. "That's a lot of stuff for basic Mac."

"Who said anything about basic?" Before I could answer, he reached over and put one finger to my lips with a smile before he pointed to the camera.

The camera. Right.

Antonio stood tall and squared his shoulders as he fixed his Bad Boy Chef smile into place, the one I had watched for hours and hours as I cooked right along-side him.

"What I have for you today is two sets of ingredients. One for your everyday mac and cheese, and one for when you want to impress that special someone, or even a crowd. A friend of mine will make her own everyday mac, and then I'll show you how to punch it up."

I shook my head and as soon as he paused or stopped the camera, I pointed an accusing finger at him. "Forget it, Antonio. No way am I cooking and definitely not on camera." The last thing I needed was the whole damn internet seeing my extra ten pounds which would probably look like twenty on camera.

"First of all," he practically purred at me, "you're beautiful, and my viewers would be lucky if they got a chance to set eyes on you while you cooked. Second, you won't cook it on camera, you just have to eat it on camera. And moan like you love it."

I gave him a skeptical look. "Since when did your show become R-rated?"

"Since I first heard you eat." His wide grin was so earnest, my breath hitched at the heat in his voice. "Now, get cookin', woman."

I glared at him but slid off the stool and we switched places. I used the distraction of cooking to ignore Antonio until he made it impossible. Two blocks of cheese had to be shredded which meant I didn't have to look at him.

"How's Oliver? I wonder if he is why you can't forgive me for something I haven't done."

His question was...astute. Surprisingly, so and I gave him honesty in return. "Probably. But in fairness to Dad, it wasn't just him. He was just the first man to choose something or someone else, over me. He wasn't the last, though."

"Shit." The word came out on a gruff breath and he shook his head. "That's rough."

"Yep. And there is nothing to forgive you for, Antonio. We've been over this."

"Yeah, we have. I don't need to be forgiven but you want nothing to do with me?"

It was a fair question. "If we spend time together, we'll end up in bed together."

He leaned forward, chin rested on his fist. "Tell me more," he said and wiggled his eyebrows suggestively.

I laughed because the man was too funny and charming for my peace of mind. "And that's a problem, because while I had fun with you, I realized that I'm not a *fun for the sake of fun* kind of girl." It was beyond fun being with a man like Antonio. He was sexy and sweet, and he had an unexpected depth, a passion for his career. He was exactly the kind of man a woman like me would fall for even though I knew I shouldn't. "And here we go, basic mac and cheese."

Antonio smiled when I set the first plate in front of him. "Looks and smells good." He turned and started filming again with a smile. "This is my good friend's mac. It's creamy and cheesy, well-seasoned. The touch of smoked paprika really kicks this up a notch, and I like the Irish cheddar mixed with the mozzarella." He took a bite and moaned so erotically I had to clench my thighs to stop the aching throb between them. When he opened his eyes, they gleamed with mischief. "Delicious." He took another bite and then another, until the plate was almost empty.

Antonio licked his lips and smiled at the camera.

Bastard.

"Now we'll see what we can do to turn this everyday dish into a gourmet dish."

"How was it really?"

Antonio frowned at me. "It was really good. You can make your mac and cheese for me any day of the week, Augusta. It's the perfect way to refuel between orgasms."

"Is that all you think about?"

"No," he answered seriously. "I also think about how you look in your scrubs. How the kids all love Nurse Gus because she's so friendly and treats them like grownups. I think about the way your eyes sparkle when you're challenged, and the way the pulse in your throat flutters like hummingbird wings when you're turned on. Like now."

He was right, dammit. I was turned on, and it wasn't just because of his words, or how gorgeous he looked with his face focused on the dish he created. He moved easily, but I knew every move was well thought out.

"I left you speechless," he observed with a smile. "Good."

"Not speechless, I'm just trying to figure out your goal in all of this." There had to be one, and I didn't think my limited sexual skills required this much effort.

Instead of answering, he set a beautiful plate of gourmet mac right in front of me, a cocky grin on his face.

"It's a good-looking plate." It was the plate you would expect at a restaurant that had a dress code, the kind of place I hadn't been to in far too long.

"Thanks. It's lobster and thick-cut pancetta with a garlic and herb breadcrumb topping."

I closed my eyes and inhaled deeply, the mix of scents made my stomach growl loudly. "Damn, Antonio. I'll never look at my plain mac the same."

His gaze darkened and before I realized his intent, Antonio stood beside my stool and turned me to face him before he cupped my cheeks and took my mouth with his. The kiss was hungry and intense, right from the start, like he was a man crazed for me. He deepened the kiss and speared his fingers through my hair, growling like a man out of control. His tongue teasing me, playing with me, pleasing me until I moaned.

He stepped back, dark gaze even darker as he stared at my lips, moist from his kisses. "Now, taste it and tell my viewers how delicious it is."

I glared at him. "That was low, even for you."

He shrugged and let out a loud, unapologetic laugh. "I wish I could say I was sorry, but I couldn't resist. A beautiful woman telling me how my food has ruined her for all others? A man has his limits, Augusta."

"And kissing me was what you had to do?"

He nodded slowly. "Hell yeah. And now, a couple hundred thousand subscribers will think I gave you more than gourmet lobster mac & cheese before the cameras started rolling."

He was right, damn him. I could feel how swollen my lips felt and imagined my hair looked like a man's fingers had been playing in them for hours. My skin felt hot, so I knew I had a pink flush staining my cheeks, probably my chest too, but I was too stunned to look down to confirm. Instead, I smiled and did what I promised I would do. I tasted the food and sung his praises, genuinely, as I finished off the entire plate.

But ss soon as he was done filming, I slid from the stool and ran like hell.

Antonio

I slid from my truck in the hospital parking lot with a smile. I didn't have a lot to smile about, but the way Augusta had run away from me yesterday told me she wasn't just running from me, but also how she felt about me. That gave me hope because whenever she was around, I had to fight that same urge to run. To flee from feelings I swore I would never feel again.

I wasn't ready to put a name to those feelings, not yet, but I couldn't let the connection between us go, which meant I had to make sure I was on her mind as much as she was on mine. The sun was bright and high up in the sky, another sign of hope.

"Back again?" Melanie's brows rose when I stepped through the automatic doors. "No Rosie?"

"Nope. This isn't a medical visit." Melanie was a big gossip, but she also considered herself a matchmaker which meant she would be a good ally. "Augusta around?"

Melanie flashed a wide, knowing grin and pointed up with her pen. "Pediatrics floor. She just finished rounds so you'll find her up there. Somewhere."

"Thanks, Mel."

"Good luck," she called after me with a laugh.

I would always take good luck when it came my way, but I didn't need luck where Augusta was concerned, what I needed was for her to trust me. To admit that she wanted me too.

I spotted her in the middle of an empty corridor and my feet moved faster to get to her. She didn't look up, didn't notice my approach. "You ran away from me," I accused, the sound of my voice startled her.

She glared up at me, her green eyes shooting fire in my direction. "I didn't run. I went home, where I live."

"Bull. You were running scared."

She laughed but there was no amusement in it. "Yeah? What am I scared of, Antonio?"

"The heat between us. The chemistry and the connection. I wasn't expecting either, and it scares the hell out of me too."

She wanted to argue, I could see it in the tense set of her shoulders, the defiant tilt of her head. "I'm not scared because there is nothing to be afraid of. We have chemistry, sure, but that's all we have."

"You keep telling yourself that, Augusta, but this is more than chemistry and you damn well know it." She opened her mouth, probably to tell me once again how wrong I was, but I shut her up with a kiss. Unlike yesterday's kiss, I took my time. It was long and slow and hot. I teased her lips and teeth with my tongue, kneaded her hips until they pushed against me.

I couldn't get enough of the taste of her. Chocolate, like she just finished eating some, because the taste lingered on her tongue. I couldn't get enough of the feel of her mouth against mine, the way her soft tongue danced so freely with my own. The soft little moans she made when our tongues collided drove me crazy, and when she tilted her hips toward mine, I wished we were anywhere but in a public place surrounded by children.

Shit. Children. I pulled back reluctantly and sighed, my eyes scanned her face which held the same breathless wonder I felt. "Augusta," I moaned.

She pushed at my chest, frustration replacing arousal. "I'm at work, Antonio!"

"No one saw us. Would it be a problem if they did?" Was she ashamed of her attraction to me? Did she want to keep us a secret?

Augusta nodded. "Yes, it would. We're not together,

and I don't want anyone to think I'm getting my hopes up for more, only for them to see you making out with your ex on camera. I work here, and the last thing I need is for my coworkers to look at me with pity."

"Pity? Are you delusional, or just this scared?" The fear swimming in her green eyes told me the answer. "Oh my god, you *are* that scared." I couldn't believe it. "I thought you were so strong and so brave, tough and scared of nothing. But you're scared of this, of us, of how you feel when we're together. It terrifies you."

"It doesn't," she insisted in a shaky voice.

"It does, and that's okay because it scares me too. I just thought you were stronger than me."

She let out a bitter laugh. "Of course I'm scared, Antonio. I'm not your type and you don't do commitment, what kind of fool would I be to expect more from you? If I can't expect more then I can't waste my time."

"More excuses." I smiled, relieved now that I understood she was just better at hiding her fear.

"Go away, Antonio." Her words were uttered with exhaustion not rejection.

"I will, for now, but know this Augusta. I want you too damn bad to run away, so I'll be here. I'll keep showing up and I'll keep being here for you, until you believe it."

She gasped at my words.

I nodded and pressed another kiss, hard and too short, to her mouth before I pulled back with a smile.

Then I did what she asked, I turned and walked out of the hospital with a big ass grin on my face.

She was mine.

She just didn't know it yet.

Gus

❧

I stood on my father's doorstep and kicked the door with one foot because both hands were filled with grocery bags. "Dad, it's me. Open up." For just a fraction of a second, I worried when I didn't hear movement on the other side of the door. But I quickly relaxed when he yanked open the door and frowned at me.

"Augusta? Why didn't you use your key? Bangin' on my door like you're the law." His brows furrowed deep and he took one of the bags from me.

I smiled up at him. "I thought maybe you were entertaining a woman and I didn't want to catch an eyeful." He glared at me and I laughed. "Your words, not mine."

"Yeah, yeah, you're a smart-ass just like me. Come

on in. Tell me you brought me something other than broccoli and carrots."

"I did," I answered and followed him inside. "But I also brought broccoli and carrots. And cauliflower. And zucchini."

"Thank god for small favors," he growled. "And thank you for giving a damn about an old man."

"You're not just an old man, you're my dad."

He waved off my words with a grunt. "What's going on with you and Antonio?"

I blinked at the abrupt change in subject. "Nothing. Why do you ask?" I did my best to act like I didn't know what he was talking about.

Dad laughed, more like guffawed and pointed at me. "That's strange because the whole dang town is talking about how he laid one on you in the middle of the hospital. And in The Outpost parking lot. That's lots of smooching for nothing."

"That's all it was, Dad, a few kisses." Kisses meant nothing to a man like Antonio, who could have any woman he wanted. He took them for granted and I refused to read the emotions I felt in those last two kisses, because they were one-sided.

He didn't feel the want, the need, the desire to know more. To be more. He wanted the physical and nothing else. He cherished his bachelorhood more than he wanted me, and I had to accept it.

If I knew why I wasn't worth the effort, that might make it easier. "Dad, can I ask you a question?"

"Anything. Shoot."

"Why didn't you try to give up drinking for me?"

His gaze shifted downward, guilt tugged at his features.

"It's not an accusation, Dad. I just want to know. Please?" I was a medical professional, so I knew it wasn't just that easy, but maybe he had some insight that I didn't.

Dad sighed and turned a sorrowful gaze in my direction. "I was too deep in my own misery and my own depression to save my own life. I wanted to, more than anything, for you. Only for you. Every time I looked into your sad eyes, I wanted to do better. To be better. Hundreds, maybe thousands of times, I wished I was that man, the one who could just kick the habit and give you the upbringing you deserved. I just wasn't strong enough."

I listened carefully, and mostly what I heard was just how hard things were for him. That he wanted his drink and his misery more than he wanted me. "I understand, Dad."

"Do you? Because I don't think you do." He shook his head and rubbed a hand over his grey hair. "Addiction is powerful, and no matter how much I wanted it, I wasn't ready. I hadn't hit rock bottom yet. That didn't happen until you finally left my sorry ass to fend for myself."

"I had to." I'd stuck around for as long as I could because someone had to take care of the house and the bills, but it got harder and harder.

"I know it, and I'm glad you did. Would've been so much worse if you had sacrificed your future for me, when it wasn't clear I would have one."

I never let myself think of how bad it must have gotten before he finally went to rehab and stopped drinking. I didn't want to know. "I'm glad you're better, Dad."

He shook his head. "Every damn day is a struggle and I imagine it will be for as long as I'm able to draw air, but when I wake up clean and sober, I smile because it means I conquered another day." He walked to me and wrapped me in his wiry arms and gave me a tight squeeze. "Don't let my failures as a father cost you future happiness, sweet Gus. Antonio is a good man who wants nothing more than to be a good father to his daughter."

"I know that, Dad." The problem wasn't that he wasn't a good man, that had never been the problem.

"Then what's the problem, girl?" Dad frowned at me like I was the crazy one. That stung.

"I can't trust him with my heart. He lied to me once and I refuse to wait around for him to realize what he really wants is his ex, or a woman just like her." A man like him didn't go from a Hollywood beauty to a frumpy nurse, no matter what he thought. No matter what anyone else said.

"You forgave me. Can't you forgive him too?"

I shook my head. "I don't think so, Dad."

"Why the hell not?"

I sighed. I didn't want to talk about this, not with him, because it would only hurt him. "Because Dad, my childhood scarred me. I have a habit of choosing men who need me because, I guess I think it means they'll stay for as long as they need me. But they don't. Not ever." It was pathetic, how much I twisted and contorted myself to be loved in the past. I was older now, which meant I should be wiser. I wasn't wise enough not to fall for Antonio, but I had to be wise enough to not give in to those feelings.

"Well I am sorry about that, but sweetheart you're smart and beautiful and any man would be lucky to have your love. I know I'm a lucky bastard that you still talk to me, and even now, you're still taking care of me." He smacked a rough kiss to my cheek. "Even if all you bring me is vegetables."

"Old habits die hard," I assured him with a warm smile.

"Well, kill that habit and bury it ten feet under." He stomped his foot on the floor for good measure. "And there's something else, Antonio doesn't need you. He's been taking care of him and his little girl without you for years. If he wants you, it's because he just wants you."

A nice thought, but I still didn't trust it. "I don't know about that."

"Well you should think on it, long and hard," he said with a smile as the doorbell rang. A quick look at the watch on his wrist produced a wicked smile. "Not too long though, that's probably Antonio and Rosie here for lunch." His loud belly laugh echoed behind him as he went to open the door.

"Damn scheming old man," I growled to myself and put on my game face.

I could do this, spend an hour or two with Antonio without thinking about more. Without wanting more than he would ever give.

Antonio

The surprise in Augusta's eyes when I walked into the kitchen, matched my own, so lost in my thoughts as Rosie and I made the short walk to Oliver's little ranch house, I didn't notice her car parked out front.

"Augusta. Hi."

"Hey," she shot back a little breathlessly. Her eyes stayed on my face, almost as if she was happy to see me. Almost. Then her gaze darted to Rosie and Oliver, and her shoulders fell. "I'll let you all get to your afternoon as soon as I put away the groceries."

"Stay," I insisted automatically. "There's room for all of us. Right?" Maybe she just didn't want to be around me, but part of my plan was to make that impossible.

"Of course." The words came out on a haughty tone

that brought a smile to my face. "What have you got planned?"

My smile brightened. "Brought some ginger beer and strawberry soda for Ollie here, the old man can't get enough."

"Who you callin' old, boy? I'll still give you a run for your money," he griped but I didn't need to look over to hear the smile in his voice.

"Ginger beer?" I could her thoughts swirling, the fear that instantly darkened her eyes.

"It's fermented, but nonalcoholic. I wouldn't do that."

Augusta blinked rapidly and shook her head. "I know that. It's just, habit, I guess." She shrugged off the moment of worry that seemed to take her back to her childhood and tried for a smile that did nothing to mask that moment of terror. "So, what else?"

"Fresh ground lamb for burgers along with a cherry mint relish and tzatziki sauce. Homemade hotdogs with a new ketchup I'm working on. Veggie kabobs. Tons of stuff for a barbecue and more than enough for all of us."

She eyed the food set out on the counter and nodded. "You're the chef, so I'll be out of your way in a sec."

"Come on, Rosie. Let's go get the grill started," Oliver took her hand. "I'll even let you toss the match in."

"All right!" She put her hand in his and they exited through the kitchen into the backyard.

It was just me and Augusta. "I don't want to interrupt time with your dad, Augusta. We can go."

"No need. He invited you over and I just showed up." She turned to the fridge and took her time putting the food away. "I can handle this if you can," she said when she turned back to me, her tone defiant, a challenge.

"I can more than handle it, because I want to see you and talk to you. I want to be around you."

"Antonio," she sighed.

I didn't want to get into another argument, so I unpacked the food and changed the subject. "The mac & cheese episode goes live today. Want to watch it together?"

A cascade of red curls swung around her face and shoulders when she shook her head. "Absolutely not. If I decide to watch it, I'll do it by myself."

My lips curled into a grin at her words. "Why do it by yourself when you can do it with company?" I wiggled my eyebrows and she stared at me for a long moment before a laugh exploded out of her.

Was there anything more lovely, sexier, than a woman who laughed with wild abandon? Her shoulders shook, her tits jiggled and her skin flushed beautifully as she laughed. I didn't even care that it was at my expense.

"What?"

"You're gorgeous," I answered simply because it was the truth. The sun that filtered into the kitchen through the blinds lit locks of her hair like fire.

"I'm not," she insisted just as I knew she would.

"You have a problem, Augusta, you know that?"

She folded her arms and her auburn brows crinkled in confusion. "Oh yeah, what's that?"

"You're blind, or rather you don't' see what I see when I look at you." Maybe living in LA had left me jaded, but it seemed impossible that a woman as beautiful and smart and appealing as her, couldn't see it. "That's okay, I'm perfectly happy to show you what I see."

The back door smacked open and Rosie rushed inside, interrupting the moment. "Daddy, can I split a strawberry soda with Grandpa Ollie?"

Augusta froze at Rosie's words and I wondered what that was about. "Rosie, you know he's not really your grandpa, right?" Big, worried green eyes looked to me for help, but my daughter had it under control.

"I know, but my grandpas don't live here, and Grandpa Ollie said he could be my grandpa and do grandpa things with me, like take me out for ice cream, give me strawberry soda and dollars. Lots and lots of dollars." Her matter-of-fact tone, as if it was just a foregone conclusion, was damned adorable.

Augusta thought over Rosie's words, smiled and

shrugged. "Cool. The logic is sound and it never hurts to have more people love you. What a lucky girl you are." I watched the openness, the honesty on her face, left me transfixed.

She was that way with everyone but me.

Rosie smiled before she launched herself in Augusta's arms. "Love you too, Nurse Gus." She squirmed away, the call of strawberry soda too strong, and darted towards the door and turned to me. "Can I Daddy?"

I nodded. "That means you can't have one with lunch."

"Okay." She smiled again and ran to the backyard.

"She is a little whirlwind."

I laughed. "An accurate description, though I would have said tornado, some days a gale force wind." Her wistful smile tugged me closer, a magnetic pull I couldn't resist. "You sure you're okay with her calling Ollie, Grandpa?"

She frowned up at me. "Of course. I just wanted to make sure she didn't think so because of us. That could be confusing. Or hurtful."

"Thank you, for thinking of her heart."

She shrugged off my words, but the move wasn't dismissive. "She's an amazing little girl."

"You're good with kids."

Augusta let out a small laugh and shook her head. "I've worked with children for years, I should hope so."

Her words were slightly dismissive but it was more than that and I smiled. "What?"

"I'm learning more about you with every word out of your pretty little mouth."

She pushed away from the counter and folded her arms. "What's that?"

"You are horrible at taking a compliment, like spectacularly awful at it."

"Am not," she insisted childishly.

"Are too," I shot back because I couldn't resist. Her lips curled into a smile in response to my own and I turned back to seasoning and shaping the burgers in front of me. "Platter?"

She disappeared into the walk-in pantry and reappeared with several serving trays and busied herself with them. "I can take a compliment just fine," she said grumpily as she lined each tray with parchment paper. "I just don't appreciate pretty words the way most women do, because in my experience, they lack substance."

"Believe me when I tell you that I think you are beautiful. Gorgeous. Stunning. And sexy. Smart and kind. And sexy."

She smiled and a small blush stained her skin. "You said that already."

I shrugged. "It's true. Twice."

Augusta rolled her eyes. "See? Pretty words from a man who's ex-wife is professionally beautiful."

"Trishelle is pretty on the outside, sure, but it's only on the outside." She stared at me, studied me, as if trying to figure out if I meant what I said, and I let her look. "You're pretty everywhere. All over." She laughed again and I spent the rest of the afternoon working to hear that sound again. "You'll see Augusta."

Gus

❧❦❧

"Y̲ou'll see. That's what he said," I sighed and looked across my kitchen table at Megan's smiling face, a box of pastries between us and an iced tea pitcher beside it. "What in the hell does that mean?"

"I'm not completely sure, but Antonio is right. You really don't see how wonderful you are." She shook her head, dark ponytail swinging behind her, and reached for a lemon bar. "Maybe that's why you end up with jerks and losers, and not because of your need to take care of everyone. Men see that you don't know how wonderful you are and they prey on that, make you feel that you're not great, so you'll keep taking care of them."

I shook my head instinctively at her words but they gave me pause. Was that true? Had I been blaming my childhood and my dad for my terrible choice in men when the truth was, I was just insecure? I don't really think so.

"I'm not all that great, Megan. I'm all right and that's plenty." Everyone couldn't be fabulous and beautiful and kind and all that. Some of us had to be plain and nice enough, smart enough. Just, enough.

"Wrong," she shouted loud enough to make me jump in my seat. "You are pretty damn great, Gus. You moved to this town a few years ago and already you're one of us. You pitch in when you're needed and every kid in town thinks you're the bee's knees."

"Bee's knees?"

She shrugged. "It's retro and I'm bringing it back," she insisted. "The point is that you *are* great, and the fact that Antonio knows it and wants you so badly, means he sees it too. Better than you."

"How do I know it's not just pretty words to get me in bed again?" Not that I was opposed to more sex with Antonio, but I couldn't with how I felt for him. Not now.

Megan rolled her eyes and took a long sip of spiked tea. "Men love sex, Augusta. It is just a fact of life. Casey is insatiable, he always wants it, even after hours spent in the operating room. Does that mean he only wants me for my body? No."

"You're not seriously comparing your relationship

with your childhood sweetheart, your husband, with my fling with Antonio?"

She laughed. "Why not? The outcome doesn't matter, Gus. The fact that Antonio sees you means he will value you for the woman you are, successful and stunning and smart and sweet. And sexy." She wiggled her eyebrows with the last part.

I laughed. "Did you read the 'S's' on the thesaurus toilet paper today?"

"No, smart-ass. I just figured alliteration would bring my point home better."

It worked, dammit. "Good job."

"Thanks." She flashed a wide smile and refilled our glasses. "What are you going to do about Antonio?"

"No idea." I wish I knew what the right move was, but I didn't, which meant I—probably—would do nothing.

"But you want him?" It wasn't really a question but I nodded anyway.

"I do. It's a terrible idea, but I do want him. A lot." It was a fool's errand to want Antonio, to wish things were different. I knew that. "I also want a three layer caramel cake and to be a size five." My baking skills left much to be desired and I'd been stuck at a size ten for more years than I cared to count.

Megan nodded. "The man you want desperately can help you with the cake, and his body," she said with a grin. "The rest, you'll take care of it when you're ready."

"What if I'm never ready, Megan?" If I was strong enough or brave enough, maybe I would just jump into things with Antonio and hope for the best. But I wasn't. I was scared, terrified actually, that he would break me worse than the others.

"If you're never ready, then you'll miss out on what could be something really great, or at least really hot. And worse? You'll have to watch him move on."

That was the worst part, knowing he would move on eventually, probably to a woman who was everything I wasn't, which would confirm my fears. "This sucks."

Megan laughed. "Right? But this is the sucky part, once you figure out what you want and go after it, the rest is pretty damn great."

"Spoken like a woman who has hot sex with the love of her life on a regular basis." The doorbell rang and I sighed.

"Expecting someone?"

"No," I frowned and got up. "Maybe it's cookie season," I sang and made my way to the front door.

"Oh, if so, invite them in with all the boxes!"

I laughed at Megan's sweet tooth. It made perfect sense for her to work at a bakery. I opened the door and froze at the sight of Antonio. It was the same man I'd grown used to over the past few months, bad boy sexy with tattoos and panty-dropping smile. But, gone was the black t-shirt and grey jeans, replaced with blue. Light blue denim and a deep blue t-shirt that highlighted his olive toned skin, gave it a magnificent glow in the early afternoon sunshine. *Down girl.*

"Antonio, what brings you by?" There was nothing I could do about the husky nature of my voice so I ignored it.

And that crooked smile he flashed that said he heard it too. "You. Of course."

"Damn." Megan's whispered the word loudly and when I glanced over my shoulder, I found her fanning her face. "I think I'm gonna go home, maybe see if Casey has room in his schedule for a little afternoon delight." She wiggled her eyebrows and grabbed her purse off the table beside the door. "Call me later. Much later, I hope." Then she slid past Antonio and disappeared.

Traitor.

I turned back to Antonio and smiled shyly as I took a step back. "Come in."

He stepped inside and I backed up against the wall. We stared at each other awkwardly, for a long moment. "You're here."

He smiled. "I am."

"To see me." It wasn't a question and I bit back a smile.

"Yep." That nervous smile of his was almost as hot as the cocky one, only more endearing.

I knew I was in trouble. "You've seen me, so..." I let

the word hang in the air, curious to see what he would say, or do, next.

"I see you, Augusta." His words were deep and gravelly, thick with lust as his brown eyes raked me up and down, several times. His nostrils flared with heat. "You look beautiful today."

My instinct was to deny his words, to reject them outright, but I remembered his accusation from the other day and sighed. 'Thank you, Antonio." I wore a simple denim skirt and a t-shirt from a charity run several months back. I didn't look beautiful, but I wouldn't argue.

Not this time.

He flashed a knowing smile and took another step closer before he kicked the door shut behind him. "I brought you something."

"You don't have to bring me anything, Antonio."

"I know, but I wanted to." He produced a small white box with a gold ribbon wrapped around it. "For you."

My hand shook as I accepted the gift that he seemed shy about giving, and I looked down at it. "What is it?"

"Open it up and see."

My other hand shook as I tugged on the ribbon until it unfurled, and lifted the flap on the box. "Antonio," I gasped at the sight of the small chocolates. "They're beautiful."

"Thanks. There are dozens of discards at home, damn shaky hands," he growled with a self-deprecating smile.

"Why?"

"That day at the hospital when I kissed you, your mouth and tongue tasted like you'd just finished indulging in a piece of quality chocolate. It was delicious, and all I've been thinking about is making you some."

"You made these?"

He nodded. "There are four different flavors."

I reached inside to take one and he took the box from my hand. "Hey, those are mine!"

"They are," he said softly and reached for my hand. "But I made them and I want to see you enjoy them. Completely."

I didn't know what that meant but the heat in his gaze and the clench of his jaw, rendered me speechless and I let him pull me into the living room and guide me onto the sofa.

Antonio sat beside me, body twisted so we faced each other. He set the box on the coffee table and plucked one from it with his thumb and forefinger. "Open up."

I should have argued, I should have done anything other than part my lips at his command.

"Good girl," he growled and put the chocolate on my tongue.

My lips closed around the chocolate, catching the tip of his finger in the process. I moaned as the taste exploded in my mouth, chocolate and rum and coconut. "Damn, that's good.

"Never wanted to be a piece of damn chocolate more in my life." My belly clenched at the heat of his words, his gaze.

My breath hitched and I squeezed my legs together. Tight. "Next," I demanded on a shaky breath.

Antonio's smile was dark and promising and it never left me as he reached for another. "Open up."

I did just that and stuck out my tongue.

"Augusta," he growled.

"Yes?"

"Temptress," he grunted and brushed the chocolate across my bottom lip. "Lick."

I did. "Bourbon and coffee?"

"Impressive, but it's whiskey."

"More."

He placed the candy in my mouth and I closed my lips around the chocolate and his fingers. "Mmm."

It went on and on like that, the hottest experience of my life.

Dark chocolate and vanilla.

White chocolate and key lime.

"Which one did you like best?" Antonio asked the question, his dark gaze focused on my lips.

I looked at him and, feeling bold, I smiled. "I might need a second taste before I make up my mind."

"Whatever the sexy lady wants," he pulled me into his arms a flash of a moment before his lips crashed down on mine. It was a chaste kiss at first, no tongue but full of heat as our lips collided again and again, then his tongue teased me, back and forth, back and forth until my lips tingled.

Our mouths crashed together in a mash of lips and tongues and teeth, frantic and hungry, intense and needy. Oh, so needy. His big hands gripped my shoulders and slid down my back to settle at my waist to bring me closer to him. My hands went to his face, cupped his rugged jaw that was two days past needing a shave, and I let my thumbs slide up and down his jaw, the scrape against my thumbs sent a shiver through me.

I pulled back and looked into his eyes, dark with desire and need. "Antonio," I whispered.

"I'm right here, Augusta."

He was, right here, his gaze begged me to choose him. To kiss him.

"You are," I grinned and nipped his bottom lip. In one swift move, I was on top of him, straddling his hips and deepening the kiss.

His hands slid down to my ass and pulled me right up against where he was long and hard between my thighs. I groaned into his mouth and ground against the erection that tempted me beyond all reason. We kissed like old lovers engaged in a familiar dance, instinctively we knew how to come together, how to execute the right move that would make the other just a little wilder. A little more aroused.

A little mad.

Madness was the exact right word for how I felt in that moment. Wild and reckless too, but mostly just madness. The chocolate and the man drove me to the edge, so consumed with his body and his taste, that I couldn't think straight.

It was the only explanation for the words that left my mouth next. "Nothing better than a gorgeous man and handmade chocolates."

Antonio flashed a crooked grin and stood, palmed my ass with a grunt. "Let's test that theory," he grunted and carried me to my room.

We spent the afternoon doing just that.

Antonio

Augusta stretched beside me, her tits jiggled and her hard nipples called out to me. The moan that accompanied the stretch went straight to my cock and I pulled her close.

"You trying to tempt me again, woman?" Not that it took much for her tempt me, but her reaction to the chocolates was better than I had hoped.

"Me?" Her innocent tone as she rolled her hips into me was more than a temptation. "I'm no temptation."

My hands went to her hips and a slow grin spread across my face. "We talked about your ability to take a compliment, didn't we?"

"Was that a compliment?"

I thrust my hips up and my cock slid between her damp lips. "Did it sound like one?"

Augusta arched her back with a moan. "What was the question?"

A low growl escaped and I leaned forward and wrapped my lips around one hard pink nipple. Another moan escaped her and I sucked harder. Her hips rolled again, the move covered me in moisture. "Augusta."

She moved to her knees and gripped me in her hands to guide me inside of her. "Yes? Oh yes." Her question turned into a moan and my hips thrust up, settling deep inside her pulsing heat.

My phone buzzed and vibrated on the nightstand. As tempted as I was to ignore it, I couldn't. "I have to check it."

"Go right ahead," she moaned and swirled her hips. "Don't mind me."

As soon as I had the phone in my hand, the black screen lit up again and I answered immediately. "Ollie, what's up?" My heart raced just thinking about all the reasons he would call right now.

Augusta's hips paused and I assumed she could hear her father's voice since she separated her body from mine and stared.

"Rosie is having an attack and it's bad. None of the things you said are working and I'm right worried."

I nodded and started to move off the bed, my eyes swept the room for my discarded clothes. "I'll be right over."

"No need. I'm on the way to the hospital so you may as well meet us there."

"How is she?"

There was a long pause before Ollie answered. "She's calm about the attack, but that's not all."

"What is it?"

"We were at the park and a woman claiming to be her mama showed up. Rosie got upset and we left, but the crazy damn woman followed us, even now her and the cameras with her are following behind us right now."

Shit. "Thanks for letting me know. And thanks for keeping Rosie safe."

"No problem. See you soon," he grumbled and ended the call.

Augusta was on her feet, still naked and gaze full of concern. "What's going on?"

"Rosie is having an attack and worse, Trishelle is in town and likely caused the stress that led to the attack." That damn woman was the source of all my problems.

"No!" She picked up her phone with one hand and reached blindly in the closet with the other, a whirlwind of activity that briefly distracted me. "Suzie, it's Gus. Rosie is having an attack and my dad is bringing her in." Suzie said something and Augusta nodded as she stepped into a pair of blue panties. "I know that but there's more. Antonio's ex is following them with a camera crew. He has full custody so it doesn't matter that she's the mother, make sure security keeps her away."

I blinked in shock at her words, at the vehemence contained within each syllable. Augusta was a woman who protected the innocent. "Thanks," I told her. "I didn't even think of that."

She smiled and stepped into a pair of jeans that clung to her hips and ass. "Not the first dysfunctional family I've had to deal with, believe it or not."

"Ouch, I think."

She grinned and folded her arms across the matching blue bra. "You want me to apologize or you want to get to the hospital?" Augusta put a t-shirt on and walked from the room. "I'm driving," she called out without waiting for an answer, or for me.

"My car is blocking yours," I told her when I caught up to her at the front door where she slid into a pair of sneakers.

"I'll drive your car, then. Come on. Rosie will be scared and wondering where her daddy is." She was a force to be reckoned with, forging ahead with concern only for my sick and scared little girl.

I jumped into the passenger seat and sighed. "Thank you, for being levelheaded right now."

She flashed a sweet smile and stepped on the gas a little harder than she needed to but it felt like just a couple of minutes passed before she tugged me from the car, through the hospital doors and up to the pediatric wing. My legs moved on autopilot until the sound of a girl's scream stopped them completely. "Rosie? Rosie, is that you?"

"Daddy, I'm here! Can you hear me, Daddy?" The fear and tension in her voice started my legs moving to a fast walk and then a run.

My little girl was afraid and I needed to get to her. Now.

"To the left," Augusta called behind me just as I was about to turn right.

"Daddy!" Rosie called out again and I found her room.

I stopped in the doorway as I took in the scene, and the reason for Rosie's screams. Trishelle stood against the door, a cameraman beside her, Ollie between them and my little girl, protecting her. I grabbed his camera and tossed it on the floor. "What the fuck do you think you're doing in here?"

Trishelle blinked her long lashes innocently, a small smile tipping her lips up. "I came to see my little girl."

"Without my permission? Without calling first?"

"Not in here," Augusta said, her voice gentle but firm, her hand on my arm.

I shrugged off her touch and turned back to my ex. "Well? Answer me, dammit!"

Trishelle tried to turn on the charm and sauntered

over to me, she put one hand to my chest possessively. "Are you upset with me, Antonio?"

I grabbed her wrist harder than I should have and pushed her away. "What the fuck are you doing here?"

"My daughter is in the hospital," she pouted.

"No thanks to you," Oliver added gruffly and I nodded my appreciation to the old man for keeping Rosie safe. "She was fine and dandy until you showed up and upset her."

"Antonio, please."

"You have ten seconds to get the hell out of this room and out of my sight or I'll have a judge on the phone within the hour. You are still on probation, aren't you?"

Outrage flashed in her eyes before she turned her focus to an easier target. Augusta. "What do we have here, Antonio? You got a new girlfriend," she asked with a laugh. "Banging chubby chicks, now? I told you moving back here was a bad idea."

Augusta appeared unaffected by her words but the tension in her jaw told me otherwise. I got in Trishelle's face, towered over her with a scowl. "Better than a strung out junkie who neglects her own flesh and blood. You don't even care that seeing you is why she's in the hospital now, do you?"

Her face paled at my words and I knew I hit my target. "How dare you!"

"How dare I what," I barked out a bitter laugh, "tell

the truth? I kept my word to you and I never told anyone why I divorced you, and this is how you repay me? Too bad for you."

"Antonio," she whispered in a pleading voice that didn't affect me at all. "Please."

"Stop it. Now. Both of you." Augusta stood between us and nodded towards the door. "Out of this room or it'll be out of the hospital next." Her green eyes begged me not to keep this up in front of my daughter and I pointed to the hall for Trishelle and her cameraman.

"Out. Now."

"Antonio don't do this. Please."

"Oh now you want to be reasonable? I guess that means your followers, your fans, the producers don't know that you OD'd on the sofa while our daughter almost died beside you? They don't know that the heartbroken mother thing is just an act?"

She turned to the cameraman who had his phone out, recording surreptitiously. "Seriously, Gabe?"

He shrugged. "This is gold and you know it."

"Gabe," she squealed.

"This could be great for a redemption arc," he told her, still filming unapologetically.

She turned back to me with a glare. "Why are you doing this?"

"Because, Trishelle. Because you ambushed me on the street and tried to rope me into your bullshit. Because you did it again, you showed up when you shouldn't have and upset Rosie. Look where we are and all you're worried about is your stupid fucking career."

"It wasn't me," she insisted. "That old man wouldn't let me talk to her. I'm her mother."

"Only biologically. You lost those rights, remember?"

"You won't let me forget," she scoffed, always the victim. It was never her fault, not when she overdosed, not when she screwed up. Never.

"Yet here you are, like you forgot. Again. Maybe you ought to slow down on the drugs." Her eyes were wide and red and she couldn't stay still, a clear sign she was still using.

"Maybe you're here in this shitty little town with your fat girlfriend and you just want to erase me, like I never existed." Her phony pout left me unmoved.

I leaned in close and got in her face. "Don't ever come to my town and insult it or the people I care about. The people I love." The words were out before I could stop them.

Trishelle flicked her hair over her shoulder and scoffed. "Oh please, spare me the fake outrage, you couldn't wait to get out of this town."

She wasn't wrong. At nineteen, I was eager to leave my small town roots behind me. That was then. "This might surprise you, Trishelle, but some people actually grow up. They mature and instead of partying and getting high all the time, they turn into adults with responsibilities and real relationships. They take care of their kids instead of wasting money on designer brands and too much plastic surgery."

At those last words, she looked to the camera again and sure enough, Gabe had captured it all. "I have not had plastic surgery!" She stomped her feet, a clear sign a tantrum was coming. "I wish I never met you."

"I wish I could hate you, but I'm glad you left everything that was once good about you, in Rosie. Reality TV can have the rest of you." I cast one last look at her and sighed. She wasn't worth my anger or my pity. "Rosie needs me," I told her and walked off to check on my kid.

She was curled in Augusta's lap, her little arms wrapped around her as she sniffled. Augusta whispered something in her ear that made her smile through her tears. Rosie smacked a kiss to her cheek and let Augusta dry her tears. "Thank you, Gus."

"That's what friends are for, right?"

Rosie nodded and hugged her tighter.

That's when I realized that my words to Trishelle weren't just spoken in the moment, they were true. I loved Augusta.

Holy shit, I *loved* her.

Now I just had to tell Augusta how I felt about her, and make her believe it.

Somehow.

Gus

You heard that didn't you?" Dad wore a smug, knowing smile as we made our way to the elevator that would take us to the cafeteria, a move to give Antonio some much needed space as well as make sure Rosie got her cheeseburger. "I heard it."

Yeah, I heard the words. Believe them though, was another matter altogether. "He said what he needed to say to hurt her, to get her to back off." I wouldn't let myself believe a man's overheard words, especially those said in the heat of the moment, ever again. "His words had the desired effect, Dad. That's all."

"I wouldn't be so sure." He held the elevator doors when they slid open and nodded for me to step off. "He could have said any number of things, but he chose to say that."

I nearly ran right into Cal as I stepped off the elevator. He flashed a friendly smile. "Just can't stay away from this place, huh?"

"I can and I will," I assured him. "I'm here because Rosie had an attack. Her mother showed up while Dad was watching her."

Cal's smile faded into a frown and he took a hurried step into the elevator before the doors closed. "Thanks." He smiled and gave a salute before the doors shut.

"Come on, let your old man buy you a bowl of cafeteria chili."

My face twisted into a scowl. "Only because you made it sound so appealing." The truth was that the chili was the best thing on the cafeteria menu and I had it whenever I forgot my lunch or worked a double shift.

"You grab a seat and I'll rustle up some grub." Dad's eyes sparkled with good humor as he walked away and I sighed at the image.

I never thought I'd see him smile so freely, so easily again. It was nice to have a parent again, to have my dad back, meddling and offering up misguided advice. He saw what he wanted to see in Antonio, probably because he saw himself in the man, or the version he could have been if not for the bottle.

"All right, a bowl of chili with cheddar and jalapenos for you. A chili cheeseburger for me. With extra bacon," he winked and dropped down into the seat across from me. "We can get little Rosie's burger on our way back. Now, let's talk."

"No such thing as a free lunch," I muttered and shoved a spoonful of chili in my mouth.

Dad laughed and shook his head. "I missed out on a lot of years of giving you advice so I'll do it now. Give Antonio a chance."

I shook my head. "He hasn't asked for a chance, Dad, which means he doesn't want one. Even if he did, I don't trust him or any man to stick around." That hadn't been my reality and I didn't expect it to change anytime soon.

He nodded contemplatively as he chewed, and flashed a smile before he spoke. "Has he given you a reason to doubt his staying power?" Dad laughed to himself at the unintended joke. "Sorry."

"No, he hasn't," I answered, ignoring the innuendo. "But I'm not his type. I am not the woman a man like Antonio falls for or ends up with. This thing is just, no it *was* just a fling. He said so himself."

"Bullshit," he shouted at me, punctuating the word by smashing his fist on the table. His shout drew a few stares and Dad offered up a sheepish apology before he turned back to me. "That is pure bullshit and you know it. Antonio would be lucky to have a woman like you love him. Hell, we all would. Lord knows I don't deserve your love and I'm lucky as hell to have it."

His words took some of the fire out of me and I sighed, laid my hand over his. "Dad this is our second chance and I don't want you to keep apologizing for the past. You have already and I've accepted it. I'm happy to have you in my life again."

"I missed you too, sweetheart. It's nice, having the right to know what's going on in your life. Even nicer to meddle a little." His grin was wide and full of mischief.

"The meddling I could do without."

He laughed. "Right? But it's my right as a parent. Antonio told his ex-wife that he loved you, all you can do is trust that he means it."

I knew that, logically, but my heart wasn't the logical part of me. "I've tried that in the past and so far it hasn't worked in my favor."

"Well that's how relationships work, Augusta. They all fail, until they don't."

"Is that why you haven't gotten back on the horse, so to speak?"

He nodded. "In a way, yes. But we're not talking about me right now. We're talking about you and your trust issues."

"Hey, I earned these trust issues the hard way, thank you very much." A flash of hurt appeared in Dad's eyes and I rushed to continue. "I appreciate what you're trying to do, Dad, really. But Antonio has given me no indication he loves me or wants more with me. He's a confirmed bachelor, emphasis on confirmed. I can't let myself spin fantasies just because that's what I want."

"Of course not, but what you can do is stop being so damn scared and take the leap. Aren't you women always going on about taking the lead, being in control of your love lives? This is your chance."

My chance. Those two little words filled me with hope. Could Antonio be my chance to change the pattern of making bad romantic decisions?

No, he wasn't my chance, *this* was my chance. All I had to do was choose to believe he cared about me, he wanted me for more than a night or two. Could I do that?

If you want him, you have to.

I did want him. Badly.

Then you know what you have to do.

"Thanks, Dad. I think I needed to hear that."

His lips spread into a satisfied grin. "Wouldn't mind having a few more like Rosie around to play with and spoil. Keeps me young."

I laughed and shook my head. "Real subtle, Dad."

He shrugged. "Subtlety has never been my strong suit. I'm more of a sledgehammer than a scalpel."

That was true. "Sometimes a sledgehammer is the best tool for the job."

"Exactly."

Now I just had to figure out what the hell I planned to do about it.

Antonio

***

"**D**addy, you love Gus?" Rosie's big brown eyes looked up at me expectantly, her pale skin more so against the bright pink of her smiling lips.

I looked at my daughter with a shocked expression, the question was too grown up for my little girl. "Uh, I don't know."

Rosie was not deterred. He smile brightened, adding a hint of pink to her cheeks. "'Cause I love her too!"

Great. That made things a little more complicated and the snickering laugh that came from the doorway didn't help. "Cal," I groaned. "What are you doing here?"

"I heard my favorite princess was here and I came

to check in." He winked at Rosie who held her little arms out for a hug from her favorite uncle.

"I'm okay now, Uncle Cal. Grandpa Ollie helped."

Cal looked up, a question in his eyes. "Uncle Ollie?" He mouthed the question over Rosie's head and I only shrugged. "What happened?"

"Trishelle happened," I answered with a growl. "Showed up with her cameras to make a scene. To cause trouble."

"As usual," he added knowingly. "So?"

"So," Rosie sang. "Daddy said he loves Augusta."

I held back a groan and took in Cal's all too amused expression. "Did he?"

Rosie gave an exaggerated nod. "I love her too," she whispered to Cal and turned to me. "Does this mean she's your girlfriend now? Is she gonna be my new mommy?"

That question was the exact reason I'd kept my dating life out of Jackson's Ridge and far from my desperate-for-a-mother, daughter. Augusta and I weren't ready to be stepparents. Yet. "I don't know what it means, Rosie. When I find out, I promise to let you know."

She absorbed my words thoughtfully and nodded. "Just ask her to be your girlfriend, she'll say yes." Rosie spoke with the certainty of my sister, her Aunt Teddy.

"I agree," Cal added with a laugh.

I stared at the two smiling faced huddled together

on the too small hospital bed and let out a low groan. Girlfriend felt like such a tame word for Augusta. I wasn't sure what exact label would fit, it was too soon for wife but girlfriend felt too lightweight. Too casual for what I wanted. "Shut up, Cal."

He shrugged. "It's time to man up, before its too late. Women like that don't stay single forever."

My best friend knew the exact words to say to piss me off. "You don't think I know that?" Augusta was the only damn person who didn't know how wonderful she was, and I needed to let her know, to show her, before she moved on for good. I just didn't know what telling her, showing her, looked like.

But I knew exactly who would. "Call Teddy and tell her to bring Hannah over to my place for a powwow. With food. Two and a half hours from now."

Cal folded his arms and stared at me. "Would a *please* kill you?"

"No, but I might kill you if you don't hop to it. I don't have a lot of time, Cal."

His grin was bright and wide, a knowing smirk in his eyes. "Yeah, this was as amusing as I thought it would be."

"What?"

Cal shrugged. "Going crazy over a woman."

"I've been here before," I growled angrily as I thought of how foolish I'd been to rush into marriage with Trishelle. "Remember?"

"Yeah, I do," he said easily and stroked his chin thoughtfully. "But you weren't like this. You were bowled over by her beauty and her grind, not her."

He was right, dammit. I thought I loved Trishelle but the truth was just that I cared about her. We were both young and ambitious, and that's more than enough when you're young. It was never love, not like this. "Okay, fine. Have your fun at my expense, just get them to my house. Please."

Cal pulled out his phone and dropped a kiss on Rosie's head. "Wish your dad good luck, Princess, he's gonna need it."

She giggled at the feel of his scruff on her face. "Good luck, Daddy."

Cal snickered as he placed the call, ignoring the glare I sent him as a smile lit his face when Teddy answered. "Hey babe. Good news."

I smiled at Rosie and ruffled her hair. "Thank you, honey."

She put her little hand on my arm, stroking gently. "Don't worry, Daddy, Nurse Gus loves you too."

I wanted to believe that, however the news came to me. "How do you know that?"

"She loves everybody and you're the best so she must love you best of all."

Let's just hope that Augusta agreed.

Augusta

✦❧✦

"**W**hat do you think this means?" I stood in the middle of my living room, phone pressed up against my face while I stared at the fancy heavyweight paper in my hands, Antonio's handwriting clear as day.

Megan laughed and I could almost see her shaking her head at my question. "What exactly is *this*, Gus?"

"It's a fancy invitation with a date, place and time. It says menu but it's blank underneath. What is the meaning of this?" Hannah had delivered the invitation two hours ago. Two hours, that's how long I'd been staring at the damn paper trying to figure out what it means.

"It probably means he's inviting you to a surprise dinner. But that's totally just a guess."

"Yeah, yeah, laugh it up."

She sighed. "I'm not laughing at you, okay well I *am* laughing at you but only because you're being ridiculous. Antonio digs you, girlfriend, lean into it."

Lean into it. "What the hell does that even look like?" I spent the past week trying to figure out if I was brave enough to go after Antonio. To have him. So far, I'd come up with no answer.

"It looks like you, wearing something pretty with something sexy as hell underneath, and showing up on his doorstep looking like the knockout you are. It looks like you smiling and flirting and having a good time with a hot guy that you are totally into. Think you can do that?"

"Hell yeah." The answer came easily, without much thought.

"Then, do that. Don't wait, don't overthink it, just shower and shave, and get dolled up. Let him woo you so know that he means it."

"Woo me? Are we going for a walk around the gardens too?"

Megan laughed. "You mock, but there's a lot of sexual tension in those Regency romance novels. And yeah, if a walk around the garden with stolen kisses is what you need, do that too."

"What if this is just a case of him trying something new with the frumpy good girl?"

"First of all," she growled. "That's my friend you're calling frumpy and she's not, she's curvy and sexy and smart, and a guy like Antonio would be lucky as hell to have her love." She let out a long sigh. "Second, make it impossible for him to walk away."

"How do I do that," I asked sarcastically.

"Easy. Just be yourself, it seems to be working just fine. Now go get dressed, I'll expect full details tomorrow." Megan ended the call before I could ask the next important question.

What should I wear?

A text made the phone vibrate in my hands.

"Show of those gorgeous legs, please." Antonio.

I smiled and did exactly as Megan had advised, took a long hot shower, shave everything, and slathered myself with lavender body cream. I spritzed perfume in all the right places and took my time with hair and makeup.

This all felt important. Really important, so I took my time, carefully choosing the right shade of green eyeliner, the perfect pale pink for my lips and the pretty mint green dress I'd bought on a whim on my last shopping trip with Megan. When I was finished, I gave myself a long, assessing look in the full-length mirror and smiled.

I looked good.

Damn good, in fact.

I didn't know what this invite was all about, but I was prepared for anything, including going after the man I wanted.

The future I wanted, maybe even the one I deserved.

That thought propelled my feet forward, encased in a sexy pair of wedge espadrilles, first to the liquor store for a bottle of his favorite rum, and then on to the man himself.

My heart thudded against my chest, my hand trembled as I rang the doorbell and waited for what felt like an eternity before I was greeted by his shocked and smiling face. "Hey," I said, doing my best to sound casual.

Antonio's dark gaze was like a lover's caress as it raked up and down the length of my body. Three times. His lips pulled into a slow grin, his brown eyes full of heat. "Hey, yourself. You look beautiful."

"This old thing?" I laughed flirtatiously and swung the hem of the dress back and forth. "Thank you, Antonio."

"No, thank you, Augusta. That's just the amount of leg I was hoping for. To start." He whispered the last part in my ear as he tugged me inside the house.

As soon as he closed the door behind me, the most delicious smells made their way to me and I inhaled deeply. "It smells amazing in here. No surprise there," I added with a grin just for him.

Antonio staggered back with a wide-eyed expression. "A compliment? Maybe my horoscope was right for a change."

I blinked at his words. "You read horoscopes?"

"No. Never," he scoffed. "But today I made one up just for myself. It said a very beautiful woman would finally compliment me, and see? It came true." He winked and clasped our hands together, tugging me through the house and to the place where all the food smells lived.

"Finally? I subscribe to your channel and I always compliment your food. I think you have a selective memory." When I looked up at him, Antonio's focus was on my cleavage.

He blinked and tried for an innocent expression. "Sorry, what was the question?"

I rolled my eyes and he laughed. "You," I pointed and he only laughed harder.

"I'm right here," he replied with a smile and stepped closer to wrap his arms around my waist. "And you look gorgeous, Augusta. You smell good enough to eat," he growled. "But that's for later. Hopefully."

My body shook with need, desire burning up my veins until my temperature rose a few degrees. "What is all this, Antonio?"

He brushed a gentle, slow burn kiss against my lips. It could have lasted only a few seconds or maybe a few weeks, and I did just what Megan said I should. I leaned into it. My chest pressed against his, my hands slid around his waist and down to his fantastically tight ass, pulling a groan from him. Antonio pulled back too soon. "Some people call it dinner."

I blinked in an effort to catch up to the conversation. Dinner. Right. I looked around the kitchen and noticed the table contained a romantic dinner setting for two, complete with a single rose and small tea candle for ambience. My shoulders fell when I realized what this was.

Work.

He was filming.

I shook off the disappointment and pasted a smile on my face. "What's on the menu?"

"It's all a surprise," he answered vaguely, a proud smile on his face. "What did you bring?" He nodded toward the paper bag on the table.

"Open it up."

He did and smiled at the rum inside. "Cocktails?"

"Sure, I could go for a cocktail." I licked my lips and finally took in the sight of him. Antonio was the same man he always was, only tonight his gray jeans were accompanied by a short-sleeve black button up that still showed off his beautiful tattoos. Instead of his motorcycle boots, his feet were bare and he smelled like leather and sandalwood. And food. "You dressed up."

Surprise lit his face and he nodded. "I did. Just for you. Like it?"

I nodded. "A lot. Grown up bad boy."

He licked his lips and smacked the top onto the cocktail shaker, keeping his heated gaze on mine while he shook the silver vessel, tension heavy in the air between us. "The bad boy thing is just a marketing tool, you know."

"I do know."

"Good," he practically growled and filled two coupe glasses before handing one to me. "I wasn't sure if you would show up."

"Me either," I admitted. "But I decided that it was time to go after what I wanted."

"Me?"

I nodded. "You."

He smiled and held his glass up. "To finally grabbing the bull by the balls."

His words surprised a laugh out of me. "Sure, I'll drink to that." I took a slow sip of the cocktail and let out a low hum of satisfaction. "That is delicious."

"It's called White Empress."

"You'll have to show me how to make it." The air between us was thick with tension, but it would have to wait because he had a video to shoot.

"Or I could just make it for you whenever you want."

"That sounds, ah, nice." I swallowed down the hope and the butterflies ready to take flight as his words, at the heat when he looked at me. I wouldn't get my hopes up until I had a reason.

"Nice, huh?"

"Yep, nice." I looked at the table again and sighed. "What's the theme for today's video?"

"Romance." He set his cocktail down and took my hand in his, brushing a soft kiss to the palm. "It's the theme for the night, actually." He smiled at my short intake of breath. "Have a seat."

I smiled when Antonio held the chair out for me, like the perfect gentleman. It was sweet and his nervous smile made me want to kiss him.

But, not yet.

"Don't be nervous. I'll shoot the food and the table, then the intro and then I get you all to myself."

I shivered at his words and nodded. "Sounds good." It felt like more was going on than I was aware of, but I decided to just go with the flow. He hasn't said anything about a future so I kept my smile in place and tried to stare at the man, and not his ass encased in denim.

"Hey guys and dolls, thanks for spending another day with me, your Bad Boy Chef, Antonio." He was easy in front of the camera, calm and full of charisma. "Today we're talking about romance and I've set up the perfect night of romance for you. Want to impress your lady for your anniversary? Wow your man for his birthday? This table contains everything you need to impress that special someone."

He paused to film the table, giving me direction for

what to do with my hands, when to take a sip of my cocktail and whatever else he needed. His deep, commanding voice hit me in all the right places and I knew no matter what happened after tonight, I would spend this night in Antonio's bed.

One last time.

Or the start of something great.

"Details for everything from the candle holder to the vase and the tablecloth are in the description box below, with links." He smiled and I smiled in return because, damn, he was a natural. "This is the perfect meal, period, but especially when you want to tell the woman you want more than your next breath, that you're ready to take things to the next level with her." His eyes found mine, deadly serious with a hint of a smile curling his lips.

Expectation was heavy in his gaze and I didn't know what to say. "Antonio," I whispered. I didn't know what he was saying, exactly, but I had a feeling he was saying exactly what I wanted him to say and I was, kind of, freaking out.

"Yeah, Augusta, I'm talking to you."

"Me?" I blinked and shook my head. "You want to take things to the next level?"

He nodded.

"With me?"

"There's no other sexy redheaded nurse who has my

full attention." He wore a playful smile on his lips. "It's you, Augusta. You are the woman I want."

Hell yes. I nodded slowly as his words sank in. "What do you want me for, Antonio?" I needed him to be honest and clear. Explicitly clear.

"Where do I start?" He grinned and took my hand in his, pressed it against his chest so I could feel that this moment was special for him too. "I want you for, hell for everything. I love that you love your job, that it fires up the passion you have for people, for life and for helping others. I want you for your friendship and your smart mouth, because you don't bow down to the celebrity chef I used to be. I love that you appreciate me as a chef and a father, more than my pretty face."

"It is very pretty," I added with a laugh I barely heard over how loud my heart banged around in my chest.

"Thanks. I want you for my woman, Augusta. I want you as a partner in my life, my sounding board, I want to protect you, I want to hold you when you cry at sappy movies or scary movies. I want you to help me teach Rosie to become the woman she was meant to become. I want you in our bed each night, under me, on top of me, in the shower. I want you any and every way you want to give yourself to me, Augusta. Mostly though, I just want you."

His words were heartfelt and sweet. They weren't eloquent but they were his words, straight from his heart and that meant more to me than anything. "Antonio, I want you too."

He nodded. "It's not just about want, Augusta. I need you. I love you."

Love. He...wait, he loves me? "You do?"

His smile was sweet and patient. "Yeah, I love you, Augusta. Is that so hard to believe?"

I shrugged. "I couldn't let myself believe that."

"And now?"

I blinked away the tears and gave his chest a smack. "Now you've made me cry on camera, in front of your hundreds of thousands of subscribers." I swiped a tear away and sighed, pressing my palm back to his chest.

"Anything else?"

"Yeah, there's something else." I stood and slid my hands from his chest up to cup his jaws. Before I said anything, I needed a taste of those lips. I kissed him slowly, heat pooling between my thighs and turning my blood to thick, hot lava. When I pulled back, his hands tightened on my hips. "You might be a bad boy chef, Antonio, but you're a really good man."

"I am?" The surprise in his voice only made him more endearing and I pulled him closer to brush another kiss to his lips.

I nodded and smiled wider. "Even better than that?"

He licked his lips and nodded. "What's that?"

"You're my man."

"Damn straight," he growled and pulled me flush

against him. His kiss was more like a possession, deep and demanding. He was in full control of sending me spiraling totally out of control. My body vibrated with want and with need, and I let out a small cry of disappointment when the kiss ended.

"Damn straight, indeed."

He laughed and kissed one corner of my mouth, and then the other. "Augusta."

"Antonio." I pressed my forehead to his and ran my thumbs along the hard edges of his jaw.

"Yes, Augusta?"

"I love you too." I did love him, fully and with my whole heart, and now I cold completely and totally, lean into it.

"Damn right you do," he growled and kissed me again. This time the kiss didn't end. It was a kiss unlike any I had ever experienced in my life, it was hot and all-consuming.

I never wanted it to end.

It ended too soon when Antonio pulled back and kissed me again. "I love you too, Augusta."

Excellent. "I just have one question for you."

His brows arched comically in anticipation.

"Before or after dinner?"

With a growl, Antonio scooped me in his arms and carried me out of the kitchen and to his bedroom, where he spent the night showing me just how much I meant to him.

How much he loved me.

Loved. Me.

It was perfect.

"I think I left the camera rolling." Antonio laughed and shook his head, held me close. And tight. "Hungry?"

I nodded. "Starved."

Even the cold romantic dinner was perfect.

Absolutely perfect.

THE END

PREVIEW: KISSING THE DR

My childhood sweetheart.
My best friend.
My wife.
She doesn't remember me.
Maybe my kisses will remind her of what she means to me, and the passion that once blazed between us.

Megan

❧

"Morning, babe."

The words came out around a yawn as I stretched and enjoyed the sight of my husband, Casey, in striped pajama pants and nothing else. The muscles in his back, honed from a youth spent rock and mountain climbing, bunched with every move. Despite spending his days inside an operating room, he had an impressive sun-kissed tone I envied as much as I lusted after it.

"Something smells good." I inhaled deeply and took in his welcoming smile.

"I haven't started the coffee yet, Megs." The amusement in his tone made me smile.

"Must be you, then." I walked into his arms and buried my face in his chest, taking another breath that was nothing but Casey. The love of my life. "Yep, definitely you."

He wrapped his arms around me and squeezed with a grunt. "Morning, sweetheart. Sleep okay?"

I shook my head, face still buried in his chest. "I would've slept better in your arms." Sleeping in an empty bed was difficult, and I hated it.

"I know." He groaned and dropped a kiss on my forehead before turning his attention back to the coffee pot. "The overnight shift isn't my favorite, but Suzie is determined that every doctor does their part, including me. Just another week," he promised.

"Nine days," I corrected with a shrug. "Gus and Persy have both said they're happy not to be on that rotating schedule."

Casey laughed. "I can go into nursing or general medicine, if you prefer?"

I rolled my eyes. "After all those years apart while you finished up medical school and then a neuro fellowship? I don't think so, mister. We'll just have to get up close and personal when we can." I tilted my head up and puckered for kiss, and my man did not disappoint.

Kissing Casey always felt like that first time. Okay, not the *very* first time we kissed in the second grade on a dare, but the first kiss that really meant something, when he was fifteen and I was fourteen. It was at that age when you finally become aware of the opposite sex, or rather the appeal of them. It was then that everything between us changed. That kiss took us from friends to something more, and that something brought us to this early morning make-out session in the middle of our kitchen.

His lips brushed mine, gentle at first, but the kiss grew more intense by the second. Moments like this hadn't happened nearly enough lately, with the both of us always rushing off to our respective workplaces—Casey as a neurosurgeon at the Jackson Ridge Medical Center, me as a baker. I savored this moment of heat, of passion, this moment that belonged only to me and my husband, as his tongue swept into my mouth and tangoed with my own. He tasted like toothpaste and Casey, and it was better than coffee this early in the morning.

"Way better," I moaned when he pulled back and smacked my ass. "That's a nice way to say hello."

His lips kicked up into a crooked grin and he scrubbed a hand over his face. "I love seeing you like this, all sexy and rumpled."

"Should I bribe Suzie with chocolate chip and macadamia nut cookies? She always buys them by the dozen when I make them."

Being the best, and only, baker in town had its perks when it came to bribing the locals, coaxing favors out of them. Or, my personal favorite, getting them to keep a secret.

"I love you for the offer, but I don't think it'll work.

On the upside, I managed to get plenty of research done."

My eyes widened in surprise as the gurgling coffee pot startled a gasp out of me, and then a laugh. "That's wonderful, Casey!"

"Yeah." He shrugged. "Who knew having no patients was the key to successful research?"

"I'm proud of you, babe." I pushed up on my toes and wrapped both arms around him, kissing him because I loved him. Because I was so damn proud of the man and the surgeon he'd become. All the sacrifices we'd made, all the years apart, were worth it because his dreams had come true.

Our dreams had come true.

We kissed for a long time, the hissing coffee machine forgotten again in the heat of our passion. His hands cupped my ass and my fingers tangled in his hair as we pressed our bodies as closely and as tightly together as we could get. In a flash, I was in his arms, legs wrapped around his waist, allowing me to feel just how hard he was under his pajamas. A low growl escaped from inside of me and I deepened the kiss, smiling against his lips.

My phone beeped and vibrated on the countertop, a not-so-subtle reminder that I had no time to take this kiss to its inevitable conclusion. My shoulders fell in disappointment as I let my legs drop.

"We don't have time. Do we?"

Casey's deep laugh rumbled against me, and he smacked a final kiss to my lips before he set me on the ground. "I could make it quick, but I'd rather take my time."

A shiver slid down my spine and I smiled. "Me too."

"Coffee?"

"Yes, please." I grabbed his oat milk and my skim milk from the fridge and set them on the table beside the brown sugar before grabbing spoons. "I'm debuting rhubarb and lemon cheesecake bites today. I left some in the fridge for you."

He groaned. "Sounds delicious."

"Let's hope it tastes as good as it sounds."

New items usually went over well, but Jackson's Ridge was a small town—no one would hesitate to tell me if I missed the mark.

"I'll let you know how delicious they tasted when I wake up." He winked when he took the seat across from me and I fought the urge to climb over the table and settle in his lap, fuse our mouths together and forget our responsibilities and obligations to the outside world. "We don't have time," he laughed and pointed at me as if he knew just what I was thinking.

"I know," I groaned and took a sip from the mug. "Too bad."

"Soon," he promised.

"Hopefully," I added with a sigh because it had been too long, weeks, since I'd gotten my hands on his naked body, tasted his skin. "Our anniversary is soon, maybe we could do a sexy staycation?"

"Maybe," he said vaguely. I ignored the sting of his noncommittal attitude and took another gulp of hot coffee.

After practically chugging my coffee, I set the mug down and stood. "I guess I'd better get going. I have a busy day today. Thank you for the coffee." I dropped my cup in the sink and went back to my husband for a long kiss goodbye since he would be fast asleep by the time I finished my shower. "Love you."

"Love you more."

It was impossible for Casey to love me more. He showed me in every way possible, at least once a day. I loved him just as much, had waited for him to come back to me, not always sure that he would. When he did come back and slid his ring on my finger, it was the happiest day of my life. Our love was strong and true and real, which made it easy to ignore how disconnected we were from one another lately.

I tried not to let it bother me as I got to the bakery, unlocked the large back door, and got started on the big sellers for the day. The citizens of Jackson's Ridge couldn't get enough bread or cookies, but muffins and cupcakes flew off the shelves as well, not to mention the daily specials. The specials kept people coming in daily, which was job security for me.

That was the problem with being a baker—working

gave you too much time to think about the problems in your life, big or small. It was hard not to feel *something* over feeling disconnected from my husband, especially now that we only got to spend a few minutes together each day thanks to our schedules. He was just coming in after a long shift when I woke up to start my own.

One more week and our lives can get back to normal.

Our anniversary was coming up, but more important than that, Casey would be on a normal shift, which meant only a long surgery would keep him at the medical center later than usual.

One more week.

After putting bread in two ovens and cookies in the other two, I set a reminder on my phone and labeled it Anniversary Shopping. It was time to reconnect with Casey, and our anniversary was the perfect opportunity.

Maybe we could even use the special day to get started on expanding our family.

Casey

✿❀✿

I stood at the side of Mrs. Caperton's bed with a friendly scowl. "I am well aware that your granddaughter is the lead in the high school's production of *Rent*, Mrs. C, but you're only thirty-six hours out of surgery. You need to rest."

The older woman jutted her chin out defiantly, and her light brown eyes said she wouldn't make it easy. "All I have to do is sit there and watch her perform. And clap loudly at the end."

I sighed and gave her my best glare. "Wrong. You have to get there, deal with big crowds and the anxiety of being related to the star of the show. That's too much stress this soon after surgery, unless you want to fall down again?"

She sucked in a breath. "You know I don't."

"I don't think you do, but you're not acting like you don't, Mrs. C."

She huffed, but her shoulders fell in resignation, and she pointed two fingers at me. "You're lucky you're handsome, Casey Jackson, or else I'd take you over my knee."

I laughed and shook my head. "Tell you what, you get healthy on my schedule and if you can catch me, I'll let you."

A slow grin spread and turned into a laugh. "I guess I'll just have my daughter video it for me."

"The school might stream the opening night performance and you can see it live. At home with snacks and tea."

Surprise flashed in her eyes. "You think so?"

I nodded toward the phone. "Why don't you call the theater teacher and find out?"

"You know darn well it's the theater director, Dr. Jackson. It's the same man who directed your wife all through high school. That girl could light up a stage, and her voice. Divine."

She wasn't wrong. Megan sang like a bird, so good I was sure she'd flee town the moment we got our diplomas for the bright lights of a big city that would allow her to show off her skill. Instead, she'd stayed in town.

"You're not wrong," I agreed and tapped the foot of

her bed. "Rest up, and I'll be back in a few hours for another test."

"So many tests I feel like I'm in school again," she grumbled to herself as I walked out of her room and nearly plowed right into the hospital administrator.

"Suzie, where's the fire?"

She pushed her glasses up on her nose, stepped back, and let out a low sigh that accompanied a smile that said she was about to ask me for a favor. "No fire, I was just focused on my next task—which is you, as it happens."

Here we go. "Me?"

"Yes." She tugged on the hem of her black blazer and stood a little taller. "We have a VIP patient coming in three days and they specifically requested you."

"Okaaaaay." I drew the word out into several syllables. "And?"

She sighed. "And you know what that means. Heightened security protocols, clearing as much of the floor as we could, private OR, and a non-disclosure agreements."

"I know all that, but there's something else, right?"

"Yes, but I can't tell you."

Oh, great, one of those. "Will I have to wait until an hour before the surgery to find out what needs to be done?"

"No," she sighed. "I have everything you need in my office."

Good. "Does this mean I'm off the overnight shift?" There was no way in hell a VIP would agree to a middle-of-the-night surgery.

"In two days, it does."

"Oh, come on, Suzie. You can just screw up my schedule like that when a VIP is coming in?"

Suzie rolled her eyes. "Save it, Casey. I know you're a good surgeon, able to switch those skills on whenever they're needed. But because I'm a good administrator, tomorrow can be your last overnight shift."

"Thank you. I'll be up to see those scans as soon as I finish my post-op rounds."

She nodded and walked off, probably to talk someone else into a favor. It made her a good administrator, but it also made most of the hospital staff groan and run in the opposite direction when they saw her. She was good at her job, and I only gave her a tough time when it was necessary.

Like to get off the overnight shift.

Rounds only took about an hour and most of those were patients from outside of Jackson's Ridge, since the medical center served a wide swath of western Oregon that didn't have access to top-notch medical care. They drove from as far as a hundred miles away to get the care they needed, and I made sure none of my patients ever felt like a number, spending time chatting with them if necessary.

"Casey, hold up!"

Persy's voice echoed in the hall and I turned with a frown for Dr. Persephone Vanguard, who insisted everyone call her Persy or Dr. Persy.

She rolled her violet eyes and flashed a devilish grin. "Oh, don't look at me like that. This is the neurology department, not the library."

"What can I do for you, Dr. Vanguard?"

Her eyes narrowed but she bit back whatever retort was on the tip of her lips. "I need your assistance with a patient."

I folded my arms and grinned. "You mean, you need my expertise?"

"Not me. Bethany," she said on a sigh and handed me the tablet. "Eleven-year-old hit her head during rugby practice. Cracked it right on the edge of those metal bleachers so there was lots of bleeding, which has her folks worried. She's experiencing dizziness, nausea, and some blurred vision. Said she's sure she lost consciousness at some point, but she doesn't know for how long."

Damn. Kids were my weakness. "All right, I can lend my expertise for Bethany."

Persy smiled and patted my shoulder. "Thanks, Casey. Bethany is tough, but her mom is already talking about pulling her off the team."

I nodded as she spoke, my thoughts on the head wound rather than the family drama.

"You're not listening," she accused. "Fine, tell me what you have planned for your anniversary."

I nearly stumbled over my feet at her words. Megan had mentioned something about our anniversary the other morning, but I was dead on my feet and hadn't really paid attention. "I'm still working on it. Any ideas?"

Persy gasped and leaned in close. "You forgot?"

"I didn't forget," I growled at her. "It just snuck up on me before I was ready."

She laughed. "You and Megs are so adorable together, it doesn't really matter what you do. Maybe a throwback prom or something cheesy like that?"

I stopped and stared at her. "Who are you and what have you done with Persephone?"

She shrugged. "I just watched *Sixteen Candles* for, like, the thousandth time. One more and I get a free toaster, or something."

I let out a loud bark of laughter and started moving again. "I'll keep that idea in mind."

I wanted to do something special because Megan and I had been working too long and too hard to have any time for each other lately.

"You can even take the credit for it," she offered with a laugh and stopped outside an exam room, gesturing for me to enter first.

Thankfully, Bethany was as tough as Persy proclaimed, and she endured more prodding and X-rays in the hopes that she wouldn't have a serious injury. She didn't. Other than twenty-four hours of being checked and questioned, the little girl would take to the rugby field again, if her mother allowed it.

"Thanks, Casey."

"No problem," I told her and left the exam room just as my name was being paged to get to the ER over the intercom.

"Good luck with the anniversary thing," she called out with a laugh.

I tossed a wave over my shoulder and made my way to the emergency department to handle another consult. And that was exactly how the shift went, from one exam room to the next, checking on post-op patients, looking at scans to schedule future surgeries, and consulting on incoming head injuries.

And paperwork. Mounds and mounds of paperwork, so much of it that my eyes started to swim and I needed another cup of coffee just to get through it all. Too much caffeine—that was the real danger for doctors and surgeons, especially since hospital coffee was little more than high-octane fuel.

Eventually, the paperwork was complete, and I smiled with the knowledge that the next time I set foot inside JRMC would be my last night shift for a good long while. I couldn't wait to tell Megan the good news, but when I pulled into the driveway of the colonial style home Megan had agreed to even though she'd wanted the red Victorian a few blocks over, her car wasn't there.

She had already left.

I glanced at the clock and shook my head. "Of course." It was well after five because of all the office work, which meant another twenty-four hours would go by before I could see my wife again. Hold her in my arms.

Unless I do something about it.

As I trudged into the house and up to our bedroom, I put a quick reminder in my phone to plan something great for our anniversary. After a quick shower, I did a half-assed job of drying off before I fell into a deep, exhausted sleep.

Later. I would get to everything else later.

Megan

❧❧❧

"Thanks for dropping in at Sweet Treats. Come back soon for your next sugar fix!" I flashed a wide smile at a group of tourists who'd just finished up a hiking tour and stopped at the bakery for carbs. I kept a friendly smile fixed on my face and waved them off.

Rinse and repeat for a group of tourists who were in town to shoot the cliffs and the birds.

And another group who'd spent the past week pretending to be cowboys at a dude ranch on the edge of Jackson's Ridge.

The influx of tourists was good for business, but it meant the bakery was always busy. Always.

These days I appreciated being so busy because it gave me less time to think about things. Not that things were bad, they weren't. Things with me and

Casey were never bad; right now, they were just a little awkward. A tad distant.

Goodness, but I miss him.

A lot.

The tourists were gone, and the line filled up with the people of Jackson's Ridge eager to get a late afternoon sugar craving satisfied, or just to catch up on any new gossip over the past twenty-four hours. I smiled and chatted with everyone, exchanging small talk and answering questions about the day's specials.

"Rhubarb and lemon?" Oliver Thompson shook his head, a wide, disbelieving smile on his face. "I never heard of such a thing but I'm willing to try anything twice. I'll take two squares and one of them chocolate croissants to wash it down with, if you don't mind." He winked and leaned forward. "Let's just keep this between me and you, yeah?"

I rolled my eyes and gave him a playful glare. "You mean, you don't want Gus to know you're eating this much sugar?"

"Exactly."

"I understand," I told him, and his shoulders sagged in relief. "But I don't lie to my friends."

Oliver shrugged. "Worth a shot."

I shook my head and rang up his order with a smile, and that's when I saw him: a tall figure with broad shoulders and a thick mass of chestnut hair that I would recognize anywhere.

Casey.

He was always the most good-looking man in the room, even when he was just a boy. He was modest, had no idea he was as gorgeous as he was, and sweet as my cherry pie. Looking at him now in a worn jeans and a faded T-shirt, you'd never guess he was the golden boy of Jackson's Ridge. The great-great grandson of the town's founders, his name was emblazoned on half the businesses and buildings in town, but Casey shrugged it off as no big deal. It only made me love him more.

I handed Oliver his order with a smile and he was on his way. My heart raced at the sight of Casey standing in line, chatting amiably with every single person who stopped to say hello. He kept his distance with the women who didn't respect our relationship, but he was never rude.

Unfortunately.

"Hey, handsome."

His mouth bloomed into a wide grin, and he leaned over the counter with a flirtatious glint in his eye.

"Hello, gorgeous." Then his lips were on mine, the kiss too short but hot enough to melt my veins at the same time. "Missed you."

I practically melted at his words and leaned into him. "Missed you, too. What can I get you?"

"More of that cheesecake you left the other day. It was delicious."

I beamed at his compliment. "Thanks, babe. Anything else?"

"A big cup of hazelnut coffee, and another of those kisses if you have any left."

I tossed my head back and laughed. "I've got plenty of those stocked up, just for you." I batted my eyelashes, heat flaring. My thighs clenched and I licked my lips. "I'll bring it out to you."

He winked and brushed another kiss to my lips before he found a table near the window. I rushed through the next several orders, eager to have a few moments with Casey even if they weren't private or intimate.

"Hey, Megan, need some help up here?" The teenage part-timer poked his head out of the kitchen with a knowing grin.

"That would be great, Tommy. Casey dropped in and I could use a break."

"Go on, I can handle any stragglers and the muffins for the council meeting just went in the oven." Tommy pushed the door open and removed the heavy-duty apron he wore before replacing it with a branded Sweet Treats apron. "Go. I've got it, I promise."

"Thanks, Tommy." I took a minute to grab Casey's order and remove my own apron, making my way to his table with a swing in my hips. "Did somebody order more kisses?"

He smiled up at me and my heart fluttered. "Come

here, you." Casey wrapped his arms around me and pulled me onto his lap, kissing me like we were long lost lovers. "Damn, that's hot."

I winked kissed him again. "You're hot," I told him and took the chair across from him. "How are you?"

"Good." He sighed and rested his chin in his hand, staring at me like I was the greatest thing in the world. "I'm operating on a VIP patient day after tomorrow."

"VIP? Fancy. Do you know who it is?"

"Not yet, probably not until the day of the surgery. But I convinced Suzie that this surgery was too important to have my schedule off, and tomorrow is my last overnight shift."

I gasped, shocked and excited and happy. "Really?"

"Yep."

"That's great, Case! Now I can go to sleep wrapped up in your arms." I let out a sigh and smiled across the table, suddenly feeling lighter. Happier. Like whatever this weird funk was, it would be behind us soon enough.

"And we won't be too tired for other things." Casey wiggled his eyebrows, and the goofy move pulled a smile out of me.

"Definitely."

"What about you? What's new? How's the rhubarb cheesecake selling?"

"Fantastic!" I launched into a long, excited word salad about cheesecake bites and the big order for the

Founder's Day Festival. "It's a big opportunity and I want to do my best."

"You always do your best. Don't worry about that."

I laughed again. "You're just saying that because I keep you plied with sugar."

"Sugar *and* sex," he added with a sexy grin.

"Speaking of, I'm heading into Eugene for some pre-anniversary shopping. Should I plan something?"

"No," he growled, his face twisted into a frown. "I've got it."

I laid a wary, sympathetic hand on top of my husband's and frowned in confusion. "You've been so busy, I just wanted to take it off your plate."

He was too busy lately—too busy for me, for sex, for fun, for date night. For everything but surgery and research, and more surgery. Other than a few amazingly hot early morning make-out sessions in the kitchen, Casey didn't have time for anything.

His expression softened and he let out a long, exhausted sigh. "I know, Megs. I know, and I'm working on it. I'm planning to talk to Suzie about getting another surgeon for my department."

I smiled because I appreciated the effort, but I knew what would happen and I suspected Casey knew it, too. He was just focused on getting what he wanted because through a combination of hard work, determination, and luck, he'd gotten pretty much everything he ever wanted in life. But I did plenty of fundraising for the JRMC and I knew they didn't have the funds to add more specialists to the payroll.

An argument for another time.

"If you need to pick up anything, just let me know. I'm going the day after tomorrow. The same day as your *big* surgery."

"I'll let you know," he said, a little distracted by something.

The door to the bakery opened and I glanced over my shoulder as another two dozen tourists entered the shop, more decamping from one of those big luxury tourist buses. "I've gotta go, babe." I stood and pressed a hard kiss to his mouth. "Love you."

"Love you more," he whispered softly and gave me one last kiss—a kiss so hot and so short, it only made me want more.

A lot more.

Casey

꧁꧂

politician. I should have known that the reason I'd left the overnight shift in my rearview mirror, the reason we had to clear an entire wing of one floor, was for a damn politician. At least he was a halfway decent politician, which lessened my anger at the privileges he'd received, and the fact that the clot I was currently removing was one hell of a beast.

Instrumental rock music played in the operating room while my team and I worked like the well-oiled machine we were. I knew everything there was to know about the blood clot in his brain, thanks to the scans and three years of medical history. So far, the politician hadn't suffered any mental slips from the clot, but it had grown too much over the past year and he wanted it handled. Quietly.

After ninety minutes in the OR, I glanced at the clock on the wall and sighed. "Has Megan called yet?"

"No, Dr. Jackson. Not yet."

I knew what I sounded like—an overprotective husband, and that was exactly what I was. Megan was a confident and capable woman, but she'd headed into the city for a shopping trip and my stubborn wife had insisted on bypassing interstate traffic in favor of back roads. Of course, I worried.

There was probably nothing to worry about. She'd called the trip a "pre-anniversary trip," which meant she'd come home with a pretty dress, maybe some sexy lingerie if I was lucky. I knew I was a lucky man, getting Megan to wait for me while I was in medical school and then my residency and fellowship. Marrying Megan was the best thing I ever did, even though things were a little strained right now because of my new research and our recent upgrade to a Tier I neuro-surgical facility. My career was going better than I had ever imagined, but the price was feeling too far removed from my wife.

My childhood sweetheart.

My best friend.

"How are things, Dr. Jackson?" Suzie's voice broke through my thoughts, and I looked up before I remembered this OR didn't have an observation deck.

"Good," I assured her as I tried to keep my annoyance to a minimum. "It's taking some finesse, which means it's time-consuming, but so far, so good."

"Excellent. I'll let the family know."

I grunted a response, glancing at the clock again as worry settled in my gut. The rain had started about thirty minutes ago and those back roads were prone to flooding and accidents. "Still nothing?"

"No, Doctor."

"Dammit," I growled and turned back to removing the clot. The sound of the rain falling outside was the perfect soundtrack for this type of precision work, but as the rainfall grew thicker and more treacherous, the knot in my belly tightened.

Three hours later and it was a damn downpour outside, the clot was just about removed, and Megan still hadn't called. She should have been back in Jackson's Ridge by now and if she was, she would have checked in to ask how the VIP surgery had gone and to gush over her new purchases.

"Call again, please."

The nurse, to her credit, didn't roll her eyes or protest, she just picked up my cell phone and dialed. "No answer."

Dammit, Megan, where are you?

Five minutes later, the phone rang. "Put it on speaker, please."

"Casey? Hey, babe, how did the surgery go?" The

tension in my chest eased at the sound of her upbeat, smiling voice. "Is it a pop star?"

"No comment," I told her with a smile. "How was shopping?"

"Great," she said, a little too brightly, and I knew something was up.

"What's up, Megs?"

"Nothing," she sighed. "Well, not *nothing*, it's just a flat tire. I tried to change it myself but it's so dang wet out here that I couldn't get a proper grip on anything." She sounded so put out about not being able to change her own tire, I had to smile.

"That's why we pay for roadside assistance," I reminded her.

"I know, and I called them when it became clear I couldn't do it myself. But the rain has caused all kinds of trouble on the interstate," she emphasized the word to head off any comments I might make about her being on the interstate. "They said I'd be stuck out here for two hours. Two hours, Case!"

"It's just two hours, not a lifetime, Megs." I hoped she wouldn't do something foolish, like get out there again on a poorly lit road and try changing the tire herself. Again.

"Oh, wait, someone is stopping. Looks like a good Samaritan is going to save my tail today."

"Megs, wait! Don't just walk up to a stranger." Other than a few years of culinary training, my wife had lived her whole life in our small town. She was a bit naïve about the world at large.

She grunted. "If someone is kind enough to stop and offer help, Casey, I'm not going to turn them away and accuse them of being a psycho killer."

Light laughter sounded in the OR at her words, and I let out a low sigh to keep my frustration at a minimum. "I'm not saying to accuse anyone, just exercise some caution."

"Sure," she said, her voice a mixture of annoyance and excitement. "I'll call you when I get home. Love you to bits, babe."

"Love you, too," I muttered as the pounding rain the background stopped abruptly. She ended the call.

"Call her back in sixty minutes, please."

She would be home by then, I was sure. And it was better to be safe than sorry.

I turned back to the VIP and severed the last of the clot with ease. The surgery was a success without any early complications. I would stick around for another hour or two just to keep an eye on him and then I could go home to my wife.

At a decent hour, for once.

Yeah, things were definitely looking up.

Read the rest of Kissing the Dr here.

Also by Piper Sullivan

Midlife Baby: Morgot & Grady

Midlife Fake Out: Bella & Derek

Midlife Love Affair: Lacy & Levi

Midlife Valentine: Valona & Trey

Midlife Do Over: Pippa & Ryan

Healing Love

Dueling Drs, Book 6: Zola & Drew

Rockstar Baby Daddy, Book 5: Susie & Gavin

Unfriending the Dr, Book 4: Persy & Ryan

Kissing the Dr, Book 3: Megan & Casey

Loving the Nurse Romance: A Single Dad Romance

Falling for the Dr: A Small Town Medical Romance

Curvy Girl Dating Agency

Forever Curves: A Single Dad Romance

Small Town Curves: A Pregnancy Romance

Curvy Valentine Match: A Second Chance Romance

Misbehaving Curves: A Boss Romance

Curves for the Single Dad: A Single Dad Romance

His Curvy Best Friend: A Friends to Lovers Romance

Curvy Girl's Secret: A Baby Romance

His Curvy Enemy: An Enemies to Lovers Romance

Small Town Protectors (Tulip Series)

That Hot Night, Book 12: A Firefighter Romance

To Catch A Player, Book 11: A Second Chance Romance

Cold Hearted Love, Book 10: A Sheriff Romance

Hero Boss, Book 9: An Office Romance

Dr's Orders, Book 8: A Single Mom Romance

Mastering Her Curves, Book 7: A Curvy Girl Romance

Kissing My Best Friend, Book 6: A Fake Relationship Romance

Undesired, Book 5: A Best Friend's Brother Romance

Wanting Ms Wrong, Book 4: A Second Chance Baby Romance

Loving My Enemy, Book 3: An Enemies to Lovers Romance

Bad Boy Benefits, Book 2: A Roommate Hero Romance

Hero In My Bed, Book 1: A Roommate Hero Romance

Accidental Hookups

Accidentally Hitched: An Accidental Marriage Romance (Accidental Hookups Book 1)

Accidentally Wed: An Accidental Marriage Romance (Accidental Hookups Book 2)

Accidentally Bound: An Accidental Marriage Romance (Accidental Hookups Book 3)

Accidentally Wifed: An Accidental Marriage Romance (Accidental Hookups Book 4)

About the Author

Piper Sullivan is an old school romantic who enjoys reading romantic stories as much as she enjoys writing them.

She spends her time day-dreaming of dashing heroes and the feisty women they love.

Visit Piper's website www.pipersullivan.com

Join Piper's Newsletter for quirky commentary, new romance releases, freebies and contests.

Check her out on BookBub

Stalk her on Facebook

LOVING THE NURSE

A Single Dad Romance

❦

PIPER SULLIVAN

Enjoy Spicy Romances?

Download Safeguarded for FREE Now!

Printed in Dunstable, United Kingdom